By the same author

Death at the Yellow Rose
Fool's Gold
The Vindicators

The Forgivene

After spending forty years in pris
commit, Ezekiel Cartwright has jus
sets out to track down the men w
them, before he dies, that he has f

So begins one of the strange
tale of a man who set out on th
finds that forgiving the men pr
have guessed and, before it is ;
to take up a gun again and de
so cruelly wronged him all th

The Forgiveness Trail

Brent Larssen

A Black Horse Western
ROBERT HALE

© Brent Larssen 2016
First published in Great Britain 2016

ISBN 978-0-7198-1982-7

The Crowood Press
The Stable Block
Crowood Lane
Ramsbury
Marlborough
Wiltshire SN8 2HR

www.crowood.com

Robert Hale is an imprint
of The Crowood Press

Typeset by Catherine Williams, Knebworth

Printed and bound in Great Britain by
CPI Group (UK) Ltd, Croydon CR0 4YY

CHAPTER 1

It was a grey, chilly day in early February and the darkening sky seemed to hang low over the Georgia town of Milledgeville, as though a vast sheet of lead was suspended just above the rooftops. Why those being set free from the Milledgeville Gaol should always be released at four in the afternoon, nobody knew. It was simply the custom and had been since time out of mind. The wicket-door, set in the forbidding iron gates of the penitentiary, opened and with no external sign of ceremony, nor any indication that this was in any way a momentous occasion, an old man slipped quickly through the narrow door and out into the street which ran past the building. The door slammed shut behind him with a metallic finality that sent an involuntary shudder through the man. After forty long years, he was free.

When he had entered prison, Ezekiel Cartwright had been a handsome, strapping young fellow; a mere twenty-two years of age. Now, he looked like a grey ghost, with that bleached and unwholesome look that comes only with long years of captivity. He had passed through the gates of Milledgeville Gaol at a time when telegraphy was in its infancy and canals had been the primary means of conveying goods from one place to another. Now, railroads spanned the continent and even in his cell, Cartwright had heard the astonishing news that it was possible for one person to talk to somebody in another city, via the medium of what was known as a 'telephone'. He had been incarcerated in the year of the Forty-Nine Gold Rush and now, like Rip Van Winkle, was being turned out into a world which the frantic pace of change had rendered wholly unrecognizable.

As the old man stood there on the sidewalk, looking around him, a passerby tutted irritably, saying, 'You're blocking up the way there, old-timer! Why don't you do your dreaming at home in your bed?' Ezekiel Cartwright turned his eyes upon the impatient pedestrian, but said nothing. The man palpably flinched at the sight of this grim-looking apparition. Had this been a Catholic country, he might have crossed himself and mumbled, 'Madre Dios!', but, being an American, he contented himself with saying, 'Sorry, friend. You just come out, huh? Sorry.' Then he hurried on, as though Cartwright might be the carrier of some deadly bacillus.

Over two hundred miles from Milledgeville, on a sprawling farm lying near to the foothills of the North

Georgia Mountains, two middle-aged men were sitting at their ease in comfortable chairs. They had lately finished a pot of coffee and were now smoking as they looked through various newspapers and magazines. At length, one of them gave a low whistle of surprise and said, 'Well, I'm damned! They're letting Ezekiel Cartwright out of gaol. Can you believe it, after all these years? Why, he must be in his sixties now. I wonder why they're bothering; he can't be long for this world.'

His companion said idly, 'What does it say?'

'Let's see. Ah, yes. "Readers of a certain age may perhaps be astonished and, even after all these years, somewhat grieved, to hear that Ezekiel (Zeke) Cartwright, the so-called—"'

'Lord, that reporter surely has a flowery style,' cut in the other man. 'Just get to the nub of it.'

'They're letting him out on the … why, this very day. He'll be on the streets of Milledgeville, like as not, as we speak.'

Dave Tanner, the man who had spotted the news of Zeke Cartwright's impending release, which had been hidden away in an obscure corner of the *Fort Crane Agricultural Gazette; Incorporating the Lumpkin County Advertiser,* was thirty-six years of age that year. He was a spare-framed and supremely fit man, who ran the farm on which he lived with an iron discipline. The man to whom he had imparted this interesting snippet of news was his childhood friend Jack Lawrence, who was a year younger than Tanner. The two men still spent a good deal of time in each other's company, which was more or less inevitable, since they were close neighbours.

'D'you think it signifies?' asked Jack Lawrence, 'after all this time, I mean. You don't suppose he'll come here?'

'For revenge? I don't see it. After forty years in gaol, he must be like a wraith, I should think. 'Sides which, it wasn't any of our doing, when all's said and done.'

'Happen you're right.'

'Still, after all this time. I thought he might've been dead by now. Seems not. Hey, let's not us tell the old folk, hey? No point stirring them up and worrying anybody.'

Forty years earlier, before either David Tanner or Jack Lawrence had been born or thought of, four tough-looking men, all about the forty mark, had been sitting on a little hill not far from Fort Crane. It was a baking hot day in late summer; the sky that deep, cerulean azure which makes it a joy to be alive. The four of them were companionably passing round a bottle containing some kind of ardent spirits and as they slowly became inebriated, the men plotted robbery and perhaps murder.

'We needs must stop any foolishness from any o' them folk in the bank,' said Pat Seldon, who was as close to a leader as they had. 'Best way of achieving that end is to show folk 'fore we properly get started, as you might say, that they best not resist. Show 'em they best mind what we tell 'em to do.'

One of the men was a half-breed who went, for reasons which he had never deigned to explain, by the name of Jimmy Two Fists. This man, whose jaundiced and bitter view of the world was remarkable even among these cynical types, grunted and said, 'You mean kill one? Or more?'

'You got scruples, Jim?' asked another of the men smilingly. 'Why, you're in the wrong line of work, I reckon.'

The breed turned a cold eye upon the speaker and said, 'I don't care if we kill every mother's son in that bank. But I want to know of it beforehand.'

'I guess just one or two'll do the trick, if it comes to it,' said Seldon, 'so's the others do as we bid 'em.'

Although most people have heard of the California Gold Rush of 1849, that wasn't the first time that large reefs of gold had been discovered in the United States. The first gold rush had taken place twenty years earlier at Ward's Creek, near Dahlonega. The little town of Dahlonega in Lumpkin County, Georgia became a boom town overnight. The gold that was dug up at Dahlonega generally found its way to Atlanta, where it was stored in the only bank vault in the whole of the south at that time, on the premises of the First National Bank of Georgia. From there, it was transferred either under armed guard to Savannah, where it was exported to Europe or sent overland to the markets of Washington or New York.

Because a lot of trouble and expense went into

ensuring that shipments of gold from Atlanta were safe and not intercepted by bandits, the number of such journeys was kept to a bare minimum. It was the habit to let a certain amount accumulate in the bank vault before sending it all in one go to another location. The four men sitting and drinking just outside Fort Crane had it in mind to attack the bank, just before the next shipment was due to leave and so avoid all the inconvenience of fighting a gun battle with guards on the road out of Atlanta.

Jimmy Two Fists had been mulling over the proposals made for the raid on the bank and thought that he had spotted the weak spot. He said, 'We gwine t'Lanta. What stop they people there from shooting of us when we knock over the bank?'

'That's a good question,' Seldon remarked, taking another swig at the bottle as it was passed to him. 'What it is, is there ain't any guards at the bank. It's the peacefullest location you ever did see.'

'What's to stop anybody busting in and robbin' it then?' asked Felton Tanner, the oldest of the four.

''Cause they wouldn't stand to get much, is why,' replied Seldon. 'Only money on the premises is what there is in the tellers' drawers. Maybe a few hundred at most. The main part of the cash there and all the gold, stays locked in that there vault under the bank and's only opened at odd times. Take's two men with different keys to do it. Less'n you know when those two fellows are like to be there with their keys, then you couldn't get into that vault, even if you had a keg of powder to blow it up with.'

'So what's the game?' asked the breed. 'We sit an' wait for them as has the keys?'

'Not a bit of it,' said Seldon jovially. 'This is how we're a going to work it.'

Cartwright was having enormous difficulty getting to sleep. It was the silence that bothered him. In a prison, nights are never peaceful and quiet. There are iron-bound doors slamming shut in the distance, the tramp of gaolers' booted feet along the corridors, men shouting, others smashing up their cells, perhaps somebody who has been driven mad by the place, moaning and screaming in terror. It is a constant cacophony that you grow to live with, until it becomes part of you and its very absence is enough to deprive you of your rest.

The little lodging house in which Ezekiel Cartwright had chosen to spend his first night of freedom was, by one in the morning, as quiet as the proverbial grave. The total lack of noise made him restless and uneasy and in the end, he got out of bed and padded over to the window without troubling to put anything on his feet. It was a crisp, cold night and the moon was full, shedding its white light over the town.

When they had released him, only nine hours earlier, the prison authorities had returned to Cartwright all that he had been possessed of on his admission to

Milledgeville Gaol those many years ago. Luckily, he had kept himself trim and fit; the clothes he had been wearing still, by some miracle, fitted him. There had also been ten dollars in gold, which should be enough to tide him over for a week or two. After that, he would have to see. It didn't look likely that anybody would wish to employ a man such as him; the wrong side of sixty and a gaolbird into the bargain. It was something of a conundrum how he was going to get by and find enough to keep body and soul together.

As he stood there in the cold, gazing out the window, Cartwright thought over the scheme which had occupied him recently; seeking those who had landed him in gaol and then gone off to enjoy their lives of freedom. Wasn't he owed at least an explanation for those lost four decades of his life? He reckoned so and the sooner he straightened matters out, the better.

The next day dawned bright and clear. At breakfast, the commercial traveller with whom Cartwright shared the table was disposed to be garrulous. 'Where you heading for, pilgrim? Don't mind me sayin', you look like you could do with a vacation. I'd say you're all tuckered out by the look o' you.'

Cartwright looked at the man with mild interest, but gave no reply. This appeared to disconcert the talkative individual, for he continued hastily, 'Well, you ain't got much to say for yourself an' that's a fact! But I can respect that. It's not every man that wants to chatter away. You're a man of few words, sir.'

'More than I could say of you,' said Cartwright, before relapsing into silence. The man facing him over the table gave him an odd look, but spoke no more and they finished their meal in silence.

For the first thirty years of his sentence, Ezekiel Cartwright had been held in solitary confinement, spending all but an hour's exercise each day alone in his cell. Even the exercise was taken alone, tramping endlessly round a closed courtyard. It might have driven a lesser man out of his mind, but somehow he endured it and came out the other side healthy and sane. It was only later in his sentence, when he was allowed to participate in the ordinary life of the prison, that he heard rumours about the two former robbers who had made their fortune down in Mexico and now had one of the biggest spreads in the state. Their names were Charles Lawrence and Felton Tanner and they had once been two-bit crooks like so many of those who found their way into the penitentiary at Milledgeville. Those two, though, had struck it rich and were now wealthy land-owners and respectable citizens.

His ears had pricked up at this information, because he had, long ago, known Felton Tanner ever so slightly and would, if ever he made it out of this pestilential hellhole alive, like to pay the fellow a visit.

Fort Crane was some two hundred miles from Milledgeville and although, from all he was able to apprehend, the railroad now ran in that direction, it seemed to Cartwright that it would be a needless extravagance to travel in such style. Instead, he opted to cadge a ride on a farm wagon heading in the general direction he was going, tipping the driver a nickel for the privilege.

It was absurd, but Dave Tanner felt a little unsettled by reading about Zeke Cartwright's release the previous day. He hadn't yet mentioned the matter to his father and was reluctant to do so. Felton Tanner was, after all, eighty-three years old now. He might be as peppery and bad tempered as ever, but there was no denying that he was a very old man. It would not be a kindness to say anything that might alarm or distress him. Not that he had ever in the past shown the least sign of being bothered by the prospect of Cartwright being freed. He had never, as far as his son could recollect, ever displayed anything but contempt for the man. Which was odd, when you came to consider the matter, because all their prosperity was, in a sense, founded upon Ezekiel Cartwright.

The tract of land, covered with a farm, plantation and ranch combined, on which both the Tanner and Lawrence families lived, was vast. Felton Tanner and his good friend and business partner Charles Lawrence had acquired the land for next to nothing in the spring of 1850. On the hundreds of acres they had built two houses and lived there happily, raising their children and cultivating their property for almost forty years. Dave Tanner had been born there, as had his friend

14

Jack. Now that their fathers were getting on in years, the two younger men had more or less taken over the running of what were, nominally, two separate farms. It was a good life and anything which promised to upset it in any way, Dave Tanner saw as his business. He went in search of his friend to talk over what action, if any, it might be prudent to take.

The First National Bank of Georgia was situated on Peachtree Street. It was a grand and imposing structure; white-painted brick, with bright green storm shutters on either side of the windows. The overall impression was of a mansion on some grand plantation. The four men who had lately arrived in the city intending to plunder the bank, sat on their horses, apparently idling and smoking, but in actual fact surveying their target as shrewdly as army commanders planning a campaign.

Jimmy Two Fists was in an even worse and more disagreeable mood than usual on account of a barkeep having refused to serve him earlier that day on the grounds that he was an Indian. The breed took pride in having a white father and sometimes managed to deceive himself that others didn't guess that his mother had been a squaw. When brought down to earth, as he had been that morning, Jimmy Two Fists was apt to brood on the slight and this had the effect of making him twice as mean as was generally the case.

Patrick Seldon said quietly, so that his voice didn't

carry further than the men to whom he was talking, 'See that fellow yonder, walking on the other side of the street? Him with the eyeglasses? That's the chief cashier.'

'He don't look like he's goin' to act the part of a hero!' said Felton Tanner, which provoked chuckles from the others.

Seldon drew on the little cigar he was smoking and said, 'He'll do as the manager says. And we know *he'll* do as he's bid.'

'You sure 'bout all this, Pat?' asked Lawrence. 'I ain't a one to buy a cat in a sack, you know. You got this off certain-sure?'

Seldon turned to stare coldly at the other man and said quietly, 'You don't want in, you only got to say. You in or out?'

Faced with such a blunt choice, Charlie Lawrence backtracked swiftly. 'Hey, I ain't sayin' as I don't want in, you hear what I'm saying? Just makin' it plain. There's no doubt on any of this?'

'There's no doubt,' said Seldon.

'I don't see,' said Jimmy Two Fists, 'why I got to stay with the family. I don't like it.'

'You don't like it, hey?' asked Seldon sympathetically. 'Gee, that's too bad. You want to know why you can't come with us into the bank? I'll tell you. It's 'cause you're a damn breed is why. How many Indians you think they get in that bank in the average year? Lemme tell you, it'll be exactly none. Everyone'd mark you at once. You got shit for brains or what?'

The others noticed that the breed's face flushed deeply upon hearing the case set out so plainly. Whether Patrick Seldon observed this or not was impossible to say.

Jimmy Two Fists said flatly, 'You best watch your mouth.'

There was an awkward silence, broken by Pat Seldon saying, 'Yeah, yeah. This is nothing to the purpose. One of us has to stay with the family an' it may as well be you as another.'

Jimmy Two Fists said nothing, but continued to stare sullenly at Seldon.

They were all of them on edge and this was not the first time that hard words had been exchanged before a job. Nobody thought anything more of it until later.

CHAPTER 2

The hay cart rumbled along at a leisurely pace, with Zeke Cartwright sitting next to the man driving it. They were neither of them chatty types and so the journey passed pleasantly enough, with both men making the occasional remark and expecting nothing much in return. After they had been travelling for most of the day, the point was reached where the road to Atlanta went to the right and the destination of the fellow who owned the cart went to the left. They were by that time something in the region of twenty miles north of Milledgeville.

'Well, here's where you and me part company, fella,' said the man. 'Hope you get where you're going all right.'

'I reckon I will,' said Cartwright. 'Thanks for the ride.'

After the cart made off, Cartwright began trudging along the road north. He had no idea where he would be laying his head that night, but that was fine. He was a free man, with nobody to direct his steps anywhere in particular and that was a right good feeling, to be sure. If he was any judge, there was a good two hours of daylight left; more than enough time to find a barn or something to rest in. If not, well then that was all right too. It would do him no harm to walk a little through the night and then rest up the next day.

He had been walking for a half hour, when Cartwright heard a woman scream. The cry was cut off abruptly, as though somebody had clamped a hand over the mouth of whoever it was who had screamed. The sound had come from his right and did not sound too far away. It never crossed Ezekiel Cartwright's mind for a moment to carry on down the road and ignore what he assumed had been a desperate attempt to summon assistance.

A low dry-stone wall separated the track he was on from the neat and well-tended fields stretching away into the distance. Alongside one field was a little wood, scarcely more than a copse, and Cartwright would have taken oath that it was from there that the yell had come. For a man of his advanced years, Ezekiel Cartwright was surprisingly limber and he hopped easily over the wall and walked over to the trees to see what was going on there.

Even before he reached the copse he could see movement, as though several figures were moving back and forth and when he approached closer, he could hear snapping twigs and what sounded very much like muffled oaths. Sure as God made little apples, there was something going on there that others would rather did not become public knowledge.

Had it not been for his having heard a woman's voice, Cartwright would probably have carried on down that road and taken it that whatever was happening was no affair of his. In his book, men could most generally settle their own business without a stranger interfering and if he'd heard a man cry out, then he would not have felt any sort of obligation to investigate. Women, though, were something else again.

Threading his way through the trees brought Cartwright to a little clearing where his suspicions that there was something amiss which involved a woman were amply confirmed. Three men were doing their best to silence or subdue, he was not precisely sure which, a young woman who looked to him to be little more than a child. Over the years, Cartwright had fallen out of the habit of using his voice much and it was in consequence a little hoarse and low. Fortunately, this was not an occasion which required a whole heap of words. He said, 'What are you men about?'

In truth, the question was quite unnecessary, for it was as plain as a pikestaff what was going on. One of the men had a hold of the girl and the others had, when Cartwright had come onto the scene, been starting to remove her clothes. They looked mean, vicious types of low character. There were many such in the gaol at Milledgeville and Cartwright had over the years had his fair share of scraps and rough-houses with men like that.

The three men all looked to be young. The one holding the girl had, as Cartwright had expected, his hand over her mouth so that she could not make a noise. All of them were dressed in worn and patched clothes and it would not have surprised Cartwright to learn that they were hobos or similar; drifters moving from place to place in search of work. One of those who had been pawing at the girl and attempting to remove her clothes, turned to Cartwright with a nasty look on his face and said, 'You better stick your head in a hornets' nest, old man, than trouble us. You hear what I tell you, now?'

'Best you let that girl alone,' replied Cartwright. There was a silence after he had spoken, as though the others thought that he was going to say more. The years of solitary confinement, though, had taught him that a few words fitly spoken were worth all the pointless jabbering in the world. When it was obvious that he wasn't planning to say any more, other than advising them to free the girl, the one who had already spoken, said,

'I come over there, you goin' to be sorry. That what you want?'

And still, Ezekiel Cartwright said nothing more. In truth, there was nothing more *to* be said. He had told them to let the girl go and now he was waiting for them to do as they had been bidden. He had no desire to debate the matter further. The men were perhaps overcome with their lustful impulses and keen to get on and ravish the young woman. After saying a brief word to the one who was holding the girl securely, the other two men moved in on Cartwright.

The land which Dave Tanner and Jack Lawrence farmed was, at least in theory, divided evenly in half, making two entirely separate and distinct holdings. In practice, though, there was a good deal of overlap and the two men looked out for each other's interests.

Locally, there was a good deal of bewilderment, combined with not a little resentment regarding the amazing success of the Tanners and Lawrences. In that year of 1889, the whole country had been in the grip of an economic depression for better than a decade. Many farmers had been driven into bankruptcy by the low prices being paid for livestock and grain, but the Tanners and the Lawrences had never been riding so high. Some thought that it was due to the sheer size of their holdings; others hinted darkly that there was more to the case than met the eye and remarked meaningfully that the elder Tanner and Lawrence had in their day been notorious wrongdoers. Whatever the explanation, Dave Tanner, Jack Lawrence and their families were without doubt some of the wealthiest people in the county and, it was rumoured, perhaps among the richest in the entire state.

Early in the morning on Tuesday, 5 February, the two owners of the largest spread in Lumpkin County met together to take counsel. They were not really concerned about the unexpected release of Zeke Cartwright, but reading of him had prompted them to talk over the past and consider carefully the possible implications.

Jack Lawrence was sitting astride his horse and looking out over the fields, where a half dozen men were toiling away at removing large stones from the soil in order to facilitate the spring ploughing. When he caught sight of Dave Tanner, he hailed him, crying in a jocular fashion, 'You rose early today! It can't yet be ten.'

'Thought you and me might have a few words.'

'Sure, all you want. Draw nigh and we can exchange as many words as is needful. What's to do?'

'For one thing, we need to get down to New Orleans in a few days. There's a fresh consignment due in.'

'We can send somebody to take care of that, surely? Lord knows, we pay those agents enough as it is without running down there to check everything for our own selves.'

Dave Tanner considered this statement for a while and then said slowly, 'I'm not easy in my mind and that's the fact of the matter. I want to make sure that there's not a lot of loose talk circulating down at the docks in New Orleans. You know as well as me, we're both likely to hang if anybody finds out what's afoot here.'

Jack stirred uneasily. Then he said, 'Shit, Dave, you think I don't know that? I don't see anything coming amiss from the way we got this running. Been going well enough for I don't recall how many years now. You worry too much.'

'That's as may be,' said the other man stubbornly, 'but I ain't easy. One of us at least had best go down and look round.'

There was a silence for half a minute, as Jack Lawrence digested this and then he said, 'Seems to me like one of us at least should stop here. I been wondering about this Zeke Cartwright business. Happen it's nothing, but I wouldn't want us both off the place just now.'

'There may be somewhat in that. Well then, I'll run down to New Orleans for a day or two and see how things are shaping up at that end. You stay here and watch the old folks. I don't want either my pa or yours troubled in any wise at all.'

Jimmy Two Fists was nursing an enormous grudge; one which was bound up with the very core of his identity. The men he was riding with didn't care in the slightest degree that his mother had been an Indian, but they must have been the only people in the South who didn't. Everywhere he turned, he was met with that same unreasoning and blind prejudice which served to keep the black slaves in subjugation. He was treated as being no better than a mule or a dog; not like a man at all. It was this which led to the terrible tragedy which was ultimately laid at the door of a good-natured and carefree young fellow called Zeke Cartwright.

The plan that Pat Seldon had come up with was as simple and brutal as could be. Of the two keys necessary to open the bank vault, one presented no problem at all. The chief cashier at the bank didn't carry his key at all times, but a copy was stowed in the safe, which was protected only by an ordinary combination lock. It might need a little judicious violence, but once one of the staff could be persuaded to open the safe, then the key was theirs. The one held by the manager himself was a harder study. He only brought this to the bank at odd times, when the vault had to be opened to add or remove gold, stocks and shares or currency.

Finding a way to ensure that the manager brought his key to work on the day of the robbery had not been an especially difficult puzzle for a man as ruthless as Seldon. He ferreted around, until he discovered that Adam Booker, the manager, was happily married with a wife and three little girls whom he adored and would presumably go to any lengths to protect from harm.

Having figured out the broad brushstrokes of a crime which would quite possibly make all four of them wealthy, it remained only to find a fall guy who could be manoeuvred into taking the blame for it all. For neither Pat Seldon nor any of the other three had any doubt that after a robbery such as the one they planned, there would be the very Devil to pay and the perpetrators were likely to be tracked for however long it took to find them.

Ezekiel Cartwright, known to everybody who ever met him as Zeke, was a little down on his luck. The young man was not from Georgia, having been raised on a farm in Tennessee. He was fiddle-footed, though and in 1845, at the age of eighteen, he lit out to seek his fortune, or at the very least to have a few adventures. For four years, Zeke Cartwright roamed through Tennessee, Alabama, South Carolina and Georgia. Sometimes he had plenty of money in his pockets and other times he went hungry; but something always turned up. A few days previously, though, he had met with disaster on the road to Atlanta. His horse had taken sick and after sweating, whinnying and shivering for a few hours, had simply died. Cartwright was pretty much cut up about the matter on account of how fond he'd been of the beast. There was more to it than that, though. He was now limited in his travels to shanks's pony and that wasn't good. He would have to acquire another mount from somewhere, although how that was to be achieved, he had little idea. He barely had two dollars to his name.

After trudging wearily into Atlanta on that September day in 1849, Zeke Cartwright had an astounding stroke of luck. He fell in with two fellows who showed an interest in playing a few hands of cards for very low stakes. They had been sitting at a table outside a bar and one of them, a man who introduced himself as Stuart Bailey had hailed him as he walked by, saying, 'You look like you could do with some refreshment. Come, join us.'

Cartwright had been reluctant to accept hospitality which he was unable to repay, but very soon Bailey made him feel at ease and put forward the notion of a little poker; just for nickels and dimes. Bailey and his companion, a more taciturn type of man entirely, who went by the name of Tyler Johnson, did not appear to be very good players and even at those insignificant stakes, Cartwright soon found himself ten dollars to the good. It was in the course of casual conversation between hands, that Cartwright chanced to mention his need for a horse, together with his meagre means for satisfying this need.

'Why,' said Stuart Bailey, a smile spreading across his face, 'if that ain't the beatenest coincidence I ever did hear tell of! I can help you with that, my friend.'

'Only thing is,' confessed Cartwright sheepishly, 'the thing is where I don't have above ten dollars cash money to spend. What could I hope to get for that?'

'Well now,' said Bailey, after frowning somewhat and appearing to give the matter some little thought, 'if that ain't also fortunate. If you'd care to meet up some four miles north o' town in a few days' time, I reckon as I can accommodate you.'

Zeke Cartwright's amiable and good-natured face lit up with pleasure at hearing this. 'You could? Hey, that's right nice o' you, and me a stranger an' all.'

'Us Georgians is renowned for our hospitality to those in need. You know where the pine woods begin, four, maybe five miles north of town?'

'That place they call "The Pines"? Surely I know it.'

'Well I got business contacts up on a little ranch that way. I can not only get you a horse, but I shouldn't wonder if they couldn't be induced to furnish you with tack as well.'

This unexpected stroke of fortune was such a turnabout in Zeke Cartwright's situation, that he felt overcome with gratitude. He was a simple man and tended to take men as he found them. It wasn't that he was a fool; merely that he trusted in the essential goodness of humanity.

Even the curious circumstance which chanced before he parted company with the two men did nothing to dent Cartwright's faith in the essential kindness of this complete stranger. While reaching into his pocket for coins, the man calling himself Stuart Bailey happened to let fall a small bundle of letters. He did not notice this and so, eager to be of service, Cartwright bent down and picked up the sheath of letters. As he handed them to Bailey, Cartwright noticed to his surprise that the top letter at least was addressed not to Bailey, but rather to somebody called Felton Tanner. Still, it was no concern of his and he simply handed them to Bailey without comment.

He might have been at least twice, and quite possibly three times, the age of both the two men heading towards him, but you don't survive forty years in a penitentiary unless you are able to take care of yourself. Through his thirty years of solitary confinement, Cartwright had exercised his body religiously. Indeed, there had been little else to do and so he had devised various routines to ensure that he didn't go soft. Later on, when he was finally allowed to mingle with the other inmates at Milledgeville Gaol, he had found it vital to show all and sundry that there was no percentage in picking on him; old as he looked. He had been compelled to demonstrate his ferocity and strength regularly over the following decade, until his release.

As the first of the men came near to him, Cartwright put up his fists in classic pugilistic fashion; a move which elicited guffaws from both the other men, who were renowned among those who had dealings with them for not keeping to the usual rules of fighting. Then the guffaw turned to a shriek such as a woman might have given. While the men were focusing on the quaint and old-fashioned way in which he had raised his fists, Cartwright swung a heavily shod boot straight into the groin of the nearest man, with all the physical force at his disposal. The man's companion was distracted by the scream of pain and glanced down involuntarily at where his friend had collapsed in agony. He only took his eyes off Cartwright for the merest fraction of a second, but it was quite enough time for the older man to return his foot to terra firma and then dive forward, punching the other in the mouth with sufficient force to snap off a couple of his front teeth. This was followed up by a mighty blow to the throat, which would have felled an ox. The man dropped to the ground and lay writhing next to Zeke Cartwright's first victim.

All this had taken far less time than it takes to tell and the third man, grasping the girl to prevent her escaping, had scarcely understood what had happened, until the old man reached down and removed the pistols from the hips of his vanquished adversaries. Holding a gun in each hand, he turned to the man and girl, saying, 'You best make up your mind quickly. You want to fight as well?'

Seeing the deadly look in the fellow's eyes and the two levelled revolvers did not make the other feel at all inclined to fight. He said hastily, 'No, I throw down!'

'You carrying?'

'No, I ain't. I'm unarmed.'

'Let go that young woman and step over here to me,' said the grim-faced old man, 'I have a few words for you and your partners.'

For a moment, the man who had so far emerged unscathed toyed with the notion of using the young woman as some sort of hostage or bargaining chip. However, something about the sight of the man facing him, suggested that such a tactic might end badly and so he simply unhanded her and walked over to where his two friends lay groaning.

'When I was a young man,' said Cartwright, 'I heard of a man had his parts cut off for what you men tried. He was gelded, you understand me?' He looked hard at the man standing before him and said, 'Come closer, my voice ain't as powerful as once it was.' When the fellow was three or four feet from him, Cartwright, giving no intention of what he was about to do, suddenly swung one of the pistols hard across the fellow's face, sending him sprawling to the ground. He said softly, 'You keep your hands off women another time, less'n they're willing.' Then he turned to the girl and said, 'Tell me, where d'you live?'

'Not far from here.'

'I'll walk along of you, see you safely home.'

Cartwright's natural delicacy was such that he was uneasy about having exhibited such violence before a young lady. He said, 'I hope I didn't alarm you with my actions?'

She laughed a little shakily and said, 'Alarm me? Why, you saved me from those ... devils.'

As they walked along, Cartwright tucked the two pistols casually into his belt, giving him, if he did but know it, the appearance of a pirate or bandit leader.

As he allowed the girl to guide him in the direction in which he supposed that her home lay, Cartwright was secretly marvelling at the astonishing self-possession she was displaying. For anything that she showed to the contrary, the attempted rape by those three men had affected her not a whit. He was about to remark upon this and perhaps congratulate her on her bravery, when to his amazement she burst into hysterical tears and flung her arms around him, burying her face in his shirtfront. Of all the things that could have happened, this was certainly the most unexpected. She wept with complete abandon; like a distressed child. Hardly knowing what to do, Cartwright stroked her hair, murmuring meaningless platitudes the while, such as, 'There, there!' and, 'Don't take on, so.'

CHAPTER 3

Jack Lawrence had been more than a little disturbed by the brief conversation that he had had with his friend, neighbour and business partner. It was not that he really thought that they were in any danger, but he surely could have done without hearing about Cartwright's release from prison just now. Things had been running smoothly for seven years or so and there was every reason to hope that the next seven years would go as sweetly. There had been one or two little hiccups lately, which were nothing to get worked up about, but Tanner's reminder that they would very likely end up being hanged if the true cause of their phenomenal prosperity were to be revealed to the world had acted as a sobering reminder to him of the perilous nature of the enterprise upon which they and their families depended.

After Dave Tanner had departed, to make his preparations for the business trip to New Orleans, Jack called over one of the men working the field. 'Yessuh?' said the man obsequiously, 'How can I help you, sir?'

'By doing your damned job and not slacking while I'm away,' said Jack Lawrence roughly. 'I'm riding over to yonder bluff. But recollect that I can see you men, most all the way. Just keep at it.'

Once the boss had cantered off, the man spat in the dirt and muttered, 'Bastard!' under his breath.

Rearing up in the middle of the land owned by the Tanners and Lawrences was a towering, rocky mass; in appearance like a miniature mountain. It was about six hundred feet high and three miles in width. Sixty years ago, this bluff had been of some little significance locally, but that had long been forgotten by those who lived in the area now. It was upon this unpromising and barren-looking lump of rock that the fortunes of the Tanners and Lawrences now rested in their entirety.

When he reached Dead Man's Bluff, as it was known locally, Jack Lawrence guided his horse along a narrow and stony path which wound around the side of the craggy cliffs fringing the bluff. Although the track was well used, neither Lawrence nor Tanner had ever thought to improve it at all. It suited their purposes to leave it looking like a neglected and useless trail which led nowhere in particular.

At the top of the little path, about halfway up the side of the bluff, the way opened out to the left into a cleft in the face of the cliff. Lawrence walked his horse into this gap and then reined in. The walls of the cliff soared up a hundred feet on either side of him, leaving a narrow opening between them, which led to an open area; a kind of amphitheatre, hidden away at the heart of the bluff. Entrance to this place was hindered by a stout barbed wire fence, which was stretched from one cliff wall to the other and secured firmly in place by pitons driven into the rock face. This fence was fifteen feet high and a gate was set in it, which was secured by a large padlock. Hanging on the fence were two bright red rectangles of pasteboard, which bore skulls and crossbones. In bold, black letters, the signs proclaimed:

'DANGER OF DEATH.
SHOOTING AND BLASTING
TAKING PLACE CONSTANTLY'.

When the fence had been erected, Jack Lawrence had at first wished to put up notices which warned that, 'Trespassers will be shot'; a suggestion which had been vetoed by the more sensible Tanner, who had thought such warning more likely to arouse curiosity than discourage intruders.

After dismounting, Lawrence took from his vest pocket a little key and opened the padlock. He led his horse through, being careful to lock the gate behind him at once.

To say that Adam Booker was surprised to awaken in the middle of the night of Tuesday, 4 September 1849 and find that his home had been invaded by masked and armed men would be greatly to understate the case. 'What the Deuce is going on?' cried the general manager of the First National Bank of Georgia, leaping from the bed which he shared with his wife. He had been woken by the opening of the bedroom door and thought at first that one of the children might have come to alert their mother to a bad dream or something of that sort.

No sooner had he sprung up than Booker was knocked roughly back to the bed. The three men who had swarmed into the room were desirous of impressing upon the bank manager most forcibly that it was not in his or his family's interest for him to cut up rough.

'Listen up,' said the man who had shoved him, 'we got a proposal for you, Booker. One you might want to hear.'

By this time, Mrs Booker had also woken and she said to her husband, 'What's to do, love? Who are these men?'

'I don't rightly know,' began Booker, sitting up again, 'but I mean to find out.'

'Are you robbers?' asked Booker's wife, which prompted laughter among the men surrounding the bed.

'Robbers, Mrs Booker? We ain't robbers. We're businessmen and when once we've conducted a little business with your husband, why we'll be off out of it and you'll never set eyes on us again.'

'What do you want?' asked Adam Booker, fearfully.

'That's the spirit,' said one of the men, approvingly, 'straight to the point, that's what I like to hear! This is the way of it, Mr Booker. Me and my friends here, we aim to relieve your bank of some o' the gold as is now in the vault.' The bank manager seemed about to raise an objection at this point, but the man who was speaking held up his hand, as though to forestall this. He continued, 'I know what you're going to say. You were on the point of telling me that you'd be damned if you'd help me in any such enterprise, am I right?'

Adam Booker said nothing, but glared fiercely at the men who stood there in the darkness. The only light in the room came from the moon outside the window and the lack of light made the figures even more shadowy and menacing than would have been the case in the daytime.

'Well, we may as well set all our cards on the table here and now. You're a plain speaker and so am I. What I'll tell you is this. You screw around with us in the least degree and your wife and children will be set at hazard. There now, is that clear?'

'The children!' exclaimed Booker's wife, in a sudden ecstasy of terror. 'What's become of them?'

'Nothing. Leastways, not yet,' said the man, 'nor will anything, I'm hopeful. Well, Mr Booker? Will you play our game or bide the consequences?'

'What would you have me do?' asked Adam Booker in a low voice. The implied threat to his family had quite defeated him and he was prepared to do anything asked of him.

'That's right, you want to play it soft. I thought that'd be the way of it. Here's what we'll do. You're going to go to work this morning, same as usual. After you go, then some of us'll leave and some will stay to set a watch upon your family. Later on, we'll enter that bank of yours and you'll open up the vault for us. We'll take the gold and everybody'll be happy and you can carry on with your life.'

The implied threat hung in the air. Booker didn't need to ask what would happen to his wife and children if he failed to cooperate and the masked man offered no further explanation. It was hardly necessary. Instead, Booker said helpfully, 'There's our nursemaid and cook as well in the house. They sleep up in the attic.' He was now every bit as anxious as the robbers that all should run as smooth as clockwork in their enterprise.

Having established that the only man in the house was going to do as he was told and that the women and children would most likely follow his lead, the men who had taken over Adam Booker's home became almost jovial. This had been the crucial moment. There had always been the possibility that the bank manager might have kept a pistol by his beside or something of that nature and that might have ended in a far less agreeable situation than was now the case.

The masked men waited in the room while Booker dressed and then went with him to check that the cook and nursemaid would play their own parts without any hysterics or attempts to rouse the neighbourhood. Then, with her husband and children as hostages, Mrs Booker was given the privacy to dress alone in the bedroom. During all these activities, the children slumbered on, wholly unaware of the drama taking place in their home.

'You and me are going to take a walk down to the bank at your usual hour,' the leader of the gang told Booker. 'I'll be walking behind you, without my mask, just to make certain-sure that you get to the bank and aren't tempted to make a detour to the sheriff's office or something of the kind. Look back at me, though, so's you might recollect my face later, and I'll shoot you.'

By eight that morning, every detail was arranged and Adam Booker left the house, heading downtown to Peachtree Street. Walking a dozen paces behind him was Pat Seldon. Lawrence and Tanner then left the house at five minute intervals, with the intention of meeting up outside the bank at half past nine. Jimmy Two Fists, as had been agreed, was left in the house to guard Mrs Booker, her three daughters and the two servants. Nothing had been left to chance and the great Atlanta gold robbery would begin in less than an hour.

After the girl's racking sobs had to some extent subsided, Cartwright said, 'We best get you home. It's coming on night. Don't want to scare you, but I'd as soon have you safe at home before darkness falls. I don't rightly trust those rascals as troubled you earlier.'

This had probably been the longest speech that Ezekiel Cartwright had delivered in the last ten years or so and it left him feeling a little drained. The girl said, 'I know you're right. I'm sorry about all the weeping and so on. You must think me a regular cry-baby.'

'Not a bit of it. Let's walk as we talk.'

They exchanged names and Cartwright learned that the girl's name was Catherine Blake and that she was eighteen years of age. He gave only his Christian name and did not feel called upon to reveal his age. When they reached the little clapboard farmhouse where Catherine lived, he said, 'Your folks are at home, I reckon. There's lamps lit. I'll bid you farewell, Miss Blake. Glad I could be of service to you.'

The girl's eyes widened in dismayed astonishment and she said, 'Oh, please don't go. My father'll be so pleased to meet you.'

'I reckon not,' said Cartwright decisively. As he turned to walk away, though, the front door of the house opened and a man emerged, carrying in his hand an oil lamp.

'Catherine,' this man said sharply, 'what ails you, staying out until it's nearly dark? Come in this house right this minute, you hear what I tell you?'

On hearing her father's angry voice, Catherine began sobbing again and ran towards him, seeking comfort. For his own part, as his eyes adjusted to the twilight, Enoch Blake became aware of the man standing thirty feet or so from his door. He saw that this was a man about his own age, with two pistols tucked nonchalantly in his belt. Seeing his daughter fleeing in apparent distress from this sinister figure caused Blake to put an entirely false construction upon the situation and persuade himself that this strange-looking fellow had somehow frightened or molested his beloved daughter.

'Who the hell are you, stranger?' asked Blake angrily, 'and what have you been doing to scare my girl?'

Later on that night, Enoch Blake recalled that the most curious aspect of this confrontation, if something so one-sided could be aptly called a 'confrontation' was the absolute stillness of the man whom he had challenged. The shadowy figure stood unmoving, the fellow just staring at Blake as though waiting for him to make his move. Before Blake had gone striding over to the man to have it out with him, his daughter cried urgently, 'Pa, you got it all backwards! This gentleman saved me. He brought me home safe.'

Uncertainly, still keeping a wary eye upon the stranger, Blake went back to his daughter and she began whispering in his ear. By the time she had finished, Blake's face looked haggard and drawn in the light from the lamp he held. He said quietly to his daughter, 'Go in the house now and speak to your aunt of this. I want a few words with this fellow.'

'You ain't going to hurt him?' asked Catherine fearfully.

'Nothing of the sort,' replied her father. 'Go in the house now.'

When his daughter was out of the way, Enoch Blake walked up to the silent man, who had still not moved a muscle, and stretched out his hand, saying, 'I owe you an apology.'

'You don't owe me nothing,' said the other with a shrug. He took the proffered hand and shook it briefly, before letting it go and then turning to leave. 'I'll bid you goodnight,' he said.

'Not so hasty,' said Blake, 'I can't let a man who's done such a thing for my child, just walk off without a word. You'll at least set with us for our evening meal?'

'No, I don't think so,' said Cartwright and began moving off. Enoch Blake followed him and planted himself in front of the other man.

'My daughter is the most precious thing in my whole life,' said Blake. 'I can't let somebody who has risked his own life for her just walk off without a word. Please, come and dine with us.'

'You make too much of a trifle. Still, if it means that much to you, thanks, I could do with a bite to eat.'

Once Cartwright was in his house, Enoch Blake was able to take a close look at the man and soon realized that there was something decidedly odd about the fellow who introduced himself simply as Cartwright. For one thing, there were his clothes; they were exceedingly old-fashioned. Then again, there was that bleached-out look about his face, which to Blake's practised eye suggested at once a long spell in prison. Why did this seem to tie in with the name 'Cartwright'? There was something tickling away at the back of Blake's mind; just out of reach.

New Orleans was as bustling and full of vitality as always. Whenever he came down on business, Dave Tanner found himself half wishing that he lived not on some farm, as he did, but in the heart of a thriving, bustling city like this. There was so much life here and it made his routine existence and day-to-day life, seem a little flat and washed out in comparison.

There was so much noise and excitement in the city. The clattering and clanging of the trams, the shouting of the newspaper boys at street corners, the constant rattle of horse-drawn carriages and carts; the city never seemed to sleep. Overhead was a tangled forest of telegraph wires and there were now said to be better than a hundred telephones in New Orleans, with more being installed practically every day. There was even a rumour that the horse tram was going to be replaced soon by an electrified one; like that which had recently been set up over in Richmond. And Dave Tanner was, to all intents and purposes, cut off from this modern, new world and condemned to languish on a farm, miles from the nearest town. Little wonder then that he seized every available opportunity to come down to New Orleans whenever even the feeblest pretext presented itself to him.

One of the major expenses of the business that he ran with Jack Lawrence was the maintaining down by the docks here of a shed which contained an old Concorde stagecoach. The sight of such vehicles was now rare enough to provoke curiosity in those who set eyes upon the thing and Tanner was well aware that in another year or two it would be such an oddity that it would incite more interest than was healthy. For now, though, he didn't see that there was any other choice.

The men they used in New Orleans all had other day-to-day occupations and were paid retainers to ensure that they were available when the need arose for their services. What those occupations might be Tanner had no idea, although he strongly suspected that they probably ran to moonshining, gunrunning and rustling, rather than working in offices or stores. They were, at any rate, smart fellows who were not afraid to use violence when it was necessary.

As he had expected, two of the men for whom Tanner was looking were found in a bar, down on the waterfront. Mick Sykes and Tom Burleigh were delighted to see Tanner and welcomed him effusively. Although it was not yet midday, they were already in that expansive, alcohol-fuelled condition which is often the precursor to drunkenness.

'Tanner,' cried Mick Sykes, 'this is a rare pleasure. Come join us. What you drinkin'?'

'Nothing,' said the other man, tersely, 'and you boys best switch to soda water or pop. I want the pair of you sober.'

It was an unfortunate fact that Dave Tanner could sometimes be a little abrupt and unsociable. This didn't much matter when he was dealing with the men labouring in his fields, but had caused trouble when he adopted too high-handed an air when dealing with free men, whose help he was soliciting. Sykes deliberately took another swig from his glass of whiskey and said bluntly, 'Don't try that tone here, Tanner. It won't answer. You want our help, then we'll do it. You pay well enough. But don't try and lord it here or things'll turn sour.'

'All right,' said Tanner pacifically, 'don't take on. I meant no harm.' Inwardly, he was seething at being spoken to in this way, but both Burleigh and Sykes were an integral part of his plans and if they walked away then he didn't rightly know how he would cope. The cargo was due in within twenty-four hours and if these two men weren't here to meet it, then things could unravel mighty fast. A determined and thorough investigation could probably prove a link between the old stagecoach kept here and the farm up at Fort Crane.

'That's better,' said Sykes approvingly, 'All we ask is that you treat us as freeborn men and not your slaves.'

'Sure, sure. I didn't mean nothing. We've a cargo coming through. Ship will be docking either tonight or first thing tomorrow and you two will be needing to meet it and transfer the cargo to the stage. I have two men that will bring it up to my place.'

'How many units?' asked Tom Burleigh, who had not yet spoken.

'Six. You fellows might have to take charge of the goods 'til the stage is all ready to leave. You can manage that?'

'We ain't let you down yet, have we?' asked Sykes. 'How long you and us been working together? Been no hitches so far.'

While they were talking together, Tanner noted with irritation that the two men continued to take regular and generous sips from their glasses. There seemed little point in rowing with them, though. In a sense, Sykes and Burleigh had him over a barrel. He would be in deep trouble if they walked away from him. Not only would it be the Devil's own job to find two replacements as ruthless and efficient as those two; they knew enough between them to see him hanged. Of course, that cut both ways, but it was a powerful enough reason for him not to fall out with them.

CHAPTER 4

Pat Seldon, Felton Tanner and Charles Lawrence all drifted into the bank with every outward appearance of casualness at around twenty minutes before ten on the morning of Wednesday, 5 September 1849. They had made some effort to smarten up their appearance and looked no more scruffy or rough than many others on the streets of Atlanta. One might have taken them for farmers, come to town to draw out a little money from the bank to buy stock or something. Nothing about their external appearance shouted 'Bandits!' True, they were all three of them carrying capacious carpet-bags, but that was the only noticeable thing about them.

There were few customers in the First National Bank of Georgia that day. Two respectable-looking middle-aged men and an elderly woman, carrying a long parasol to protect her from the scorching sun, which was already indicating that the day would be a fine one, were the only people in the hall of the bank.

The chief cashier was bustling about behind the

counter, finding fault with the calculations of one of the clerks working there. Adam Booker was nowhere to be seen, although he was presumably tucked away in an office behind the door marked, 'Strictly Private'. Seldon had hoped that the bank might be entirely empty at that time of day, which would have simplified matters. As it was, two more people entered, while the three at the counter were still fooling around with some piddling little transactions. There was no point in waiting for the place to clear; they would be there all day. Seldon pulled his neckerchief up and settled it over the lower part of his face. His two companions did likewise and he then he drew his pistol and indicated to Tanner to close the street doors. It was time to commence the robbery.

At first, an element of music hall farce threatened to overwhelm the bank robbery. When Seldon tried to alert the cashier to the fact that his bank was now being robbed, the old woman with the parasol told him briskly to wait in line, like everybody else. The two men drawing out money agreed; at least until they saw the gun that Pat Seldon had in his hand. Then they fell silent and moved back from the counter, ostentatiously staring at the ground, so that the bank robbers would not think that they could later identify anybody.

The old woman took a little longer to catch the drift, continuing to argue about the fact that she had been there before the newcomer. In the meantime, Felton Tanner was standing by the door, to make sure nobody tried to make a bolt for it, while Lawrence was rapping on the door to the inner office. Almost instantly, Booker appeared, an elaborate and ornate key ready in his hand. He was plainly doing his damnedest to make sure that nobody had any excuse to harm his family.

When the chief cashier saw his boss hurrying towards him, he called at once, 'It's a theft, Mr Booker. What should I do?'

'Open up the safe, Mr Russell. We need the other key to the vault.'

'Yes sir, Mr Booker.'

Everything was, up to this point, going as smoothly as one could wish. They might have been out of that bank in another fifteen minutes with nobody hurt and no harm done to a living soul. It was not to be, though. The cashier hurried over to the safe which stood against the wall in the office space behind the counter and busied himself with opening it up in order to fetch out the other key that would be needed to open up the vault. The two male customers in the bank continued to keep their eyes fixed firmly and determinedly upon the carpet, never looking up once. It was the old woman who caused things to miscarry. She was furious that everybody appeared to be cooperating in allowing the three villains to make off with whatever they wished from the bank and so, as Seldon walked past her to make sure that the cashier was doing as expected, the old lady lashed out at him with the parasol she was holding.

If Pat Seldon had been holding a double-action piece, no harm would have been done. He would very likely just have cursed the woman and perhaps given her a shove. As it was though, he had in his hand a single-action pistol, upon the trigger of which he had already taken first pull. The parasol struck Seldon on the side of his head, causing him to twist round awkwardly. As he did so, his grip on the gun he was holding involuntarily tightened and there was an almighty crash, which echoed around the confined space of the bank. When he turned to abuse the woman for her foolish action, Pat Seldon discovered that he had quite accidentally shot her through the head.

It was a delicate moment, which under the wrong circumstances could have proved disastrous to the enterprise in which the three men were engaged. Fortunately, Seldon was not a man to be baulked by such a trifling matter as the death of a bystander. He growled at the chief cashier, who was frozen in terror. 'Just hand that key to me now, less'n you want some o' the same?'

It appeared that the cashier was not at all desirous of being shot, because he simply stood up from where he had been crouching before the safe and walked over to Seldon. He handed over the key, saying, 'Here you are, sir.'

The entrance to the vault was via a short set of steps in the manager's office. Calling it a vault was by way of being a fanciful exaggeration; it was really no more than a glorified, walk-in closet. It served the purpose well, though, of ensuring that nothing could be stolen from the bank without the willing cooperation of the staff. Leaving Tanner to cover the customers and clerks and prevent anybody leaving to raise the alarm, Seldon and Lawrence went with the manager to open the vault. They took with them both their own and also Felton Tanner's carpet-bag.

Remarkable to relate, the men who had been so unlucky as to find themselves in the bank when it was being robbed, were still gazing fixedly down at the floor. You might have thought that there was something of enormous interest about the pattern of the carpet, which was engaging the whole of their interest. The truth was they both knew that their lives were now hanging by the finest of threads. Having committed one murder, for which they would surely hang if appre-hended, what was to hinder the bandits from making a clean sweep of things by killing any possible witnesses? You could, after all, only hang once.

Seldon and the others had agreed beforehand that each of the carpet-bags could reasonably be expected to hold no more than twelve or fifteen pounds' weight. This would mean that when shared out between the four of them, each man should have something in the region of ten pounds of gold. At twenty dollars an ounce, this would mean over three thousand dollars a piece for the four of them. As it was, after they had filled the bags with gold nuggets, there was still room for a few bundles of high denomination bills as well. In one bag, they also shoved a sheath of bonds, which were utterly useless to them, looked at from a purely financial point of view. The documents were, though, crucial in their long-term plans to evade justice.

The whole raid was over in five minutes from Seldon first drawing his pistol. He and Lawrence emerged from the manager's office toting the three carpet-bags, one of which was handed to Tanner. The leader of the gang then addressed a few words to the customers and staff of the First National Bank of Georgia: 'We're leaving you boys your lives, which is more than some in our place'd do. Just be thankful. Any man pokes his head out o' the door after we go, that man'll be shot down without mercy. You all got that?'

Apparently the men left behind in the bank did get it, because it was not for some minutes that any of them dared to open the street door a crack and glance out to see if the coast was clear. The first man to leave the bank was Adam Booker. He could hardly breathe for the fear he felt for his family and simply had to get straight home to assure himself that his wife and children were safe and well.

When Enoch Blake had retired, after spending thirty years as a lawman, he felt able at last to indulge a lifelong dream and set up as a farmer. Being a sheriff had been a steady and respectable career and one more suitable, at least in Blake's eyes, for providing for a wife and child, but farming was what he had always had a hankering to do. As a lawman, he knew that a steady wage would be coming in and there were none of the uncertainties that farming entailed: poor weather, bad harvests, slumps in the price of grain and so on. Still, he had managed to save a fair amount over the years and so when he finally handed in his star, at the age of fifty-five, he knew that if he were to try his hand at farming, now was the time. His daughter was fifteen years of age at that time and Blake was not overly keen on how her life in the town was working out. He had a dreadful suspicion that she was growing a little fast.

Marianne Blake had died of the bloody flux when her daughter was but ten years of age and feeling that the growing girl would need some softening, feminine influence, Enoch Blake had invited his spinster sister to come and live with him and his daughter. So it was that in 1886, the three of them moved to the farmhouse some miles southeast of Atlanta, which Blake had purchased. And there, for the next three years, the three of them endeavoured to make a life for themselves.

Although he had worked hard at his dream, Blake had to admit that he found farming as dull as ditch-water compared with the thrill of being a sheriff. His sister was a fussy old maid, his daughter a trial and there was no escape from it all now that he was chained to the house, barn and fields. Most days he didn't travel more than a mile from the house. How he longed sometimes for the excitement of maintaining the peace and pursuing lawbreakers; never knowing from one day to the next what might befall you.

So it was that when a stranger turned up at his door after evidently having saved his daughter's life, Blake was intrigued. The fact that this man had the look about him of somebody just recently released from prison piqued his curiosity even more and made him determined to look into the man's history a little. There was, after all, nothing else interesting happening on the farm.

After being given the opportunity to freshen up a little, Zeke Cartwright joined the other three at the table. Izzie Blake served out the food and then, to Cartwright's surprise, everybody began to tuck in. He said hesitantly, 'Ain't we goin' to thank the Lord first?'

Enoch Blake looked a little irritated to be pulled up in this way and his sister coloured uncomfortably. They both, however, laid down their knives and forks. Catherine followed suit, as Cartwright bent his head and said softly, 'We thank you Lord for what we have to eat here. There's many as are going hungry and here we are with a full board. Amen.'

After this slightly unconventional grace, the other three people at the table mumbled 'Amen' and began eating again. Izzie Blake, fluttering and nervous about having a strange man in the house, especially one so grim and taciturn, said, 'Lord knows how we can ever thank you for what you did for young Catherine, Mr Cartwright. What a mercy you happened to be passing.'

Cartwright smiled faintly, but said nothing.

'Where were you heading?' asked Enoch Blake, watching the man unobtrusively, but closely, out of the corner of his eye. 'We're rather off the beaten track here, as you might say. Don't get many travellers hereabouts.'

'Do you not?' replied Cartwright, 'I can see why. You ain't exactly on a main road, are you?'

Every question put to the man was deflected, as though the guest had no interest in chatting about his business. He was polite, but not in the slightest bit forthcoming about his affairs. After the meal, as the women cleared away the wares, Cartwright stood up and thanked the family for their hospitality. It was obvious that he was about to take his leave. Blake said, 'Lord, I never did meet a fellow who was in such a hurry. Come into my study, why not, and we can talk in peace.' He called through to the kitchen, saying, 'Catherine, a pot of coffee wouldn't come amiss!'

What Enoch Blake sometimes referred to as his study and at other times his library was a small room with book shelves covering three of the walls. A desk stood in one corner and there were two easy chairs as well. Waving at one of them, Blake said, 'Sit down and make yourself comfortable.'

By the time that Blake had selected two cigars from a humidor, Catherine had arrived with the coffee. She set the pot down on the desk and then smiled shyly at Cartwright. He smiled back at her and she left the room. Blake said, 'You made a hit with her.'

'She seems like a nice kid.'

'She wouldn't thank you for calling her that!'

Zeke Cartwright accepted the cigar and allowed Blake to light it for him. Then he said, 'You fixin' to pump me? It won't answer.'

'Listen, Cartwright, let's lay down our cards and see what we got. I was a sheriff for better than thirty years. I can see you just came from gaol. You've nowhere to stay, then I'll give you a room for a few days. It's the least I can do.'

'But first,' said Cartwright, 'you want to know how long I was in for and what I did.'

'Something like that. I've the feeling that I might have come across you some time. Either met you or heard about you.'

'That's like enough to be true. Leastway, about hearing of me. Don't recollect meeting you, though.'

'So,' said Blake patiently, 'how long were you in for?'

'Forty years. I was released yesterday.'

'Forty years? My God, that must mean—'

'That I was convicted of murder?' asked Cartwright cooly, 'that's true. More than one count, too.'

For a moment, Enoch Blake wondered if he had made a dreadful mistake in inviting this old rogue into his home. Something of what was going through his mind must have shown on his face, because the man seated opposite him gave a dry chuckle and said, 'You needn't be affeared, Blake. I ain't a goin' to massacre you and your folks.'

It was the word 'massacre' that jogged Blake's memory and he knew in an instant just who it was sitting in an easy chair in his study. He said in a low, steady voice, 'You're Ezekiel Cartwright.'

'You got that right,' said the other man. 'Here I am, large as life and twice as natural. Sorry now as you invited me to set at table with you and your kin?'

After spending the day in New Orleans, checking that the old stagecoach was in good order and so on, Dave Tanner took the train back to Atlanta. He was not altogether happy in his own mind about leaving Sykes and Burleigh running that end of the operations, but couldn't immediately see what there was to be done about it. As he settled back in his seat, the train pulling out of the depot, Tanner closed his eyes and recalled with great vividness the day that he had first learned the details of how his father had made his first fortune.

It had been a couple of years after the end of the war, when Tanner had been fourteen, maybe fifteen years of age. His father's friend Charles Lawrence had come by the house and the two men were drinking late at night. When he was little, Tanner had known his father's bosom friend as 'Uncle Charlie' and he had viewed the man's son, Jack, as being a blood relative. It was only when he was a little older that he found out that the two families were not really connected in any way. On this particular night, everybody except his father and Lawrence had gone to bed leaving the two men chatting with a bottle of whiskey between them. Even to this day, Tanner didn't know what impulse had caused him to rise from his bed and come tiptoeing down the stairs to stand quietly in the hall, eavesdropping on the conversation. Maybe he had already had his suspicions about the old man's previous life.

As he stood in the darkness, the boy heard his father say, 'That poor sap has been in gaol for nigh on twenty years now, you know?'

'So what?' growled Charles Lawrence, 'he should've had more sense than to get mixed up with such a business in the first place. Who in their senses would believe that a stranger would sell him a horse and saddle for ten dollars? The man must have been simple!'

'Lucky for us, though. I can still see that stupid face of his, so pleased at getting such a bargain!'

There was silence for a spell before his father spoke once more, saying, 'It would o' eased my mind somewhat if they'd o' hanged him. Long as he's breathing, I'm never easy but that something he says might lead back to us.'

'It was that damned weakling McDermott. Worst governor this state ever did have. Commutin' all those sentences. Just our bad luck that Cartwright came up in court that year. Six months either way and he'd o' hanged for sure!'

After that, the conversation drifted off onto other topics, but young Dave Tanner had heard enough to know that his father and Jack Lawrence's too, had been mixed up in some very shady business. A man called Cartwright had somehow been cheated and then nearly hanged. The youth lay in bed, tossing and turning restlessly that night, trying to figure out what it all meant.

The day after he had heard his and Jack's father talking about Cartwright, Dave Tanner had met up with Jack Lawrence and the two boys had gone fishing together. While they sat on the river-bank, Tanner said to his friend, 'Jack, you ever hear about a man called Cartwright?'

Jack grinned and said, 'You mean Zeke Cartwright? Sure.'

'Your pa and mine were talking last night about this here Cartwright. I never heard the name before. How'd you know about it?'

'You got to swear not to let on to a living soul.'

Dave Tanner repeated the age-old formula, by licking his forefinger and holding it up in the breeze, saying, 'See that wet, see that dry? Cut my throat if I tell a lie.' Then he had waved his finger beneath his chin, in a symbolic act of having his throat cut. He said, 'Honest injun, I won't say a word. Tell me what you know.'

'My pa's got a heap of old cuttings from the newspapers, back about twenty years ago, I guess. There's this fellow called Zeke Cartwright and he was like to hang for being mixed up in killing a lot of folks. Only thing is where he didn't hang after all, on account of this new governor let him off and sent him to gaol instead.'

'Would that be Governor McDermott?'

'Hey, that's the very man! Seems to me that you know 'most as much about this as I do.'

'Only thing I don't know is what's all this to do with us. What I figure is that my pa and your'n, they somehow cheated this Cartwright fellow and he took the rap for something as they had done their own selves.'

Jack Lawrence thought this proposition over for a space and then said, his face clouded with uncertainty, 'That don't listen right. If'n that was the case, it'd mean as our pas were the ones who killed all those people in that there massacre as the papers tell of.'

'I don't see that, not no how! I reckon as that Cartwright, it was him as was the killer. Maybe our fathers just cheated him out of some horse or something at about the same time.'

Even as he had advanced this suggestion, Dave Tanner knew that that he was consciously distorting what he had heard his own father saying less than twenty-four hours earlier. It was not that Cartwright had been cheated, but rather that he had been given a horse for cheaper than should have been the case. But then, that didn't seem to make any sense, or explain why there should be a big secret surrounding the whole business.

CHAPTER 5

The five horses had been left round the back of the bank and after leaving through the main door, the three of them – Seldon, Tanner and Lawrence – walked pretty briskly round the side of the building and mounted up. They had already pulled down their masks, as they left the bank hall. There was no percentage in attracting any attention in the street. They led the spare horses as they trotted down Peachtree Street to where Jimmy Two Fists should be waiting for them.

The three riders dared not appear in too much of a hurry lest they made themselves worthy of note. Galloping hell for leather down Peachtree Street would be a sure way to ensure that folks remembered them later; the last thing they wanted. So, waiting at any moment for the alarm to be raised, Seldon and the others were forced to proceed at a steady, sedate and relaxed trot until they reached the home of the bank manager.

The breed had evidently been watching from a

window for them and he came ambling out before they had even reined in; swinging himself effortlessly into the saddle of one of the spare mounts. As they rode off towards the edge of town, Tanner took a sidelong glance at Jimmy Two Fists in order to confirm his initial impression when the man had first emerged from Adam Booker's house. He was right; the Indian's clothing was bloodstained. Not a vast amount, to be sure, but enough to suggest that somebody must have been badly hurt. There were long, dark stains down the front of the breed's pants and smaller splashes on his shirt-front and sleeves. Although he was immensely curious about the matter, Felton Tanner dreaded to ask from where the blood had come and so kept his own counsel.

Once they reached the freight yards and had crossed over the tracks, it was possible to speed up a little and the four of them accordingly broke first into a canter and then a gallop. They were keenly aware of the fact that it would not take all that long for a posse to be put together with a view to bringing them back to face justice. Actually, after killing the old woman, it would be more likely that they would be summarily hanged from the nearest tree. Either way, time was of the essence. They also needed to meet up with the young man who Tanner had befriended the previous day during the poker game. Ezekiel Cartwright had a crucial part to play yet in their plans.

When once they were clear of the town limits, the men halted briefly, so that a token amount of gold could be transferred to the saddle-bag of the spare horse they had with them. Into the bag Seldon tucked too the sheaf of papers that he had snatched up from the vault at the bank. He had no idea what they might be, but their presence in the saddle-bag served to link the owner of the horse to the robbery that had just taken place.

While Seldon was fooling around with the saddle-bag, Tanner asked the breed, 'What happened back there? Somebody get hurt?'

'What do you care?' replied Jimmy Two Fists. 'They weren't your kin or aught, were they?'

'Just askin',' said the other man, uneasily, 'it don't signify.'

They all knew what a hair trigger Jimmy Two Fists was on in the general way of things. Seeing those bloodstains prompted Tanner to think about the mood that the man had been in when they were planning the robbery. He decided to say no more about it.

They saw young Cartwright walking up and down on the edge of the pine wood as they approached. Seldon said, 'Praise the Lord! The poor young fool actually came. Well, his blood is upon his own head!'

The other three had noticed before that Pat Seldon had, from time to time, shown that he had the makings of a conscience and indicated by his behaviour that he sometimes understood that what they were doing was wrong; morally, ethically and legally. A manifestation of this was his tendency to place the blame for their misfortunes, or even their death, upon his victims.

Having helped arrange for the boy to take the rap for their own misdeeds, Seldon was now hinting that it was his own fault for being so trusting and naive.

When he saw the four riders bearing down on him, Cartwright hailed them cheerfully and addressed Tanner, saying, 'Lordy, I been waiting here a good long spell. I was beginning to think that you weren't coming.'

'Ah, I said I'd be here and so I am. Here's the horse I promised you and as you see, it's all tacked up and ready to go. You heading back to Atlanta?'

'Yes sir, that I am. Now I got me a horse, there's various bits of work I can think of taking up. I'm eternally obliged to you, I'm sure.'

While they were talking to Zeke Cartwright, the four men kept glancing anxiously down the road leading back to Atlanta. At any moment, they were expecting to see a body of horsemen riding down on them with ropes at the ready to execute summary justice upon them. It was with a sense of great relief that the transaction was completed and Cartwright took possession of the horse that they had brought him. As they prepared to ride off again at speed, the young man stopped them with a good-natured laugh. He said, 'I do declare, you are the worstest businessmen I ever did meet! Why, you all are about to dig up and leave without even taking your payment for this here horse.'

There was feigned laughter at this and Felton Tanner congratulated Cartwright on his honesty and said that it was an example to them all. Then, when once the ten dollars had changed hands, the four men reluctantly took leave of their new friend, who watched them going with a look of bewilderment on his honest and open face.

After they were a couple of miles past the Pines, Seldon called for them to rein in and dismount. Now came the most devilishly cunning part of the whole enterprise. From a sack, which he had slung over the back of his saddle, Pat Seldon produced sixteen strange-looking devices; like leather boots ending in peculiar iron shapes. The boots were split up the side, so that they could be laced up. These curious items were fitted over the hoofs of their horses. The beasts evinced little enthusiasm to be so attired, but the men were insistent. Within a few minutes, the thing was accomplished and they set off again down the road, away from Atlanta.

The boots that the horses were now compelled to wear were a scheme of Seldon's that he had had brewing for some little time. The soles of the strange footwear were iron pads which were shaped precisely like the hoofs of cattle. Anybody hoping to follow four horses would be utterly foxed by the tracks that they were now leaving. Of course, they couldn't move as fast now, for that would make the hoof prints look mighty suspicious; whoever heard of galloping cattle? But there would be no trace of the four horses that had set out from Atlanta that morning.

By contrast, the horse which Tanner had 'sold' Zeke

Cartwright had had its shoes tampered with so as to make it very easy to follow. A nail had been removed from one shoe, a mark filed across another. You would need to be stone blind not to be able to track down that creature, when once you had seen its hoof prints. All in all, the four robbers were feeling pretty braced with themselves and sure that they had made quite certain that the lightning of vengeance would descend only upon the utterly blameless head of Ezekiel Cartwright.

There was total silence in the room as Enoch Blake and Zeke Cartwright eyed each other warily. Blake broke the tension by getting up and going over to the humidor and selecting another cigar. He asked casually, 'You want another?'

'Thanks, but no. They're a little rich for me. One was plenty.'

As he carefully chose a cigar, Blake said, half to himself, 'There always was something strange about that case. I was little more than a kid at the time, seventeen, eighteen maybe, but I recall my father talking about it. You were caught red-handed and with no defence, but even so, there were those who felt you'd been railroaded.'

If he had expected the man sitting in the easy chair to burst into passionate protestations of innocence, then he was to be disappointed. Cartwright said nothing at all, but gave every appearance of listening carefully to what the other man had to say.

'I seem to remember that you were sentenced to death, but the governor commuted your sentence to life. That right?'

'Yes, that's what happened.'

'What a mercy that was for you.'

'You might say so.'

'You would rather have hanged?'

Cartwright said, 'I was sentenced in the court to be kept in solitary confinement until my execution. After Governor McDermott commuted me, the warden of the penitentiary came to see me. He said as far as he was concerned, I was to remain in solitary until my execution. That's where I stayed for thirty years.'

Blake, who knew that even a year in solitary could drive a man crazy, winced and said, 'That's the hell of a thing. Did you do it?'

'The solitary? Sure I did. What d'you mean?'

'No, I meant did you kill all those people?'

Cartwright laughed shortly. 'You know, every one of those men in Milledgeville was innocent. Why would I be any different?'

'No, really. Did you do it?'

'What do you care, Blake? I ain't a goin' to murder the man who just invited me to dinner.'

'Let's say it matters to me,' said Blake patiently. 'Did you do it?'

Long seconds passed and all Enoch Blake's instincts as a lawman of many years' standing told him that if Cartwright still refused to answer or if, even worse, he now began swearing awful oaths on his eyes or very life that he was as innocent as a newborn babe, then this would tell him all that he needed to know. In such a case, he would be certain-sure that the man sitting in his study was guilty of the most atrocious crime ever seen in the state of Georgia. In fact, Ezekiel Cartwright did neither of those things. After ten or fifteen seconds had crawled by, he said in a low, but emotion-laden voice, 'It was the foulest crime ever done and those as had any part in it at all should all have hanged. No, I knew nothing of the matter until I was arrested that day.'

Combined with what he had himself observed of the man and also his action in hazarding his own life to protect a helpless young woman, Blake was three parts convinced that Cartwright was indeed the victim of a monstrous injustice. He said, 'So what are you about, now that you're free again?'

'I'm heading over to a little town called Fort Crane. You ever hear of it?'

'Sure, I know the place. Quiet little berg. What business have you there? You got family up that way or something?'

'No. But I heard where the man who caused me to spend the greater part of my life behind bars is living up near Fort Crane. I thought I'd pay him a visit.'

'You're riding the vengeance trail?'

At this, Zeke Cartwright laughed out loud; a long rich chuckle of genuine amusement. When he'd recovered, he said, 'It's likely, isn't it? Fellow my age. No, that's not it at all.'

'What then?'

'You ain't wondered yet why they let me out of gaol, even after all these years? A man as done what they say I did? I'm dying, Blake. I have a cancer and there's nothing that any doctor can do for me.'

Blake began to offer some conventional expression of regret, but the other man waved it away, saying, 'That don't signify. I ain't looking for any man's sympathy. Don't want it, either. No, what it is, is that I've had forty years to try and figure out how come I ended in that fix. What it was all about, you take my meaning? There's no more to the case than that. Before I die, I want to speak man to man with him as condemned me in that way. See what he has to say, whether he regrets what he done. I need to make my peace with everybody 'fore I die. That's all.'

Blake mulled this over for a space and decided that it had the ring of truth. Already, the germ of an idea was fermenting in his mind; a chance for him to legitimately get away from the farm for a while and do a little detective work again. He said, 'Why don't you tell me how you first heard about the massacre and all that you know about it?'

For the first decade or so, the farms that Felton Tanner and Charles Lawrence started did extraordinarily well. The soil was fertile and rich and they had money enough to spare to buy a few slaves to help out. They prospered, began families and ploughed back the profits from the land into purchasing more slaves until, by 1861, they were flourishing as well as any such enterprise in that part of Georgia. Then came the war and, five years later, the emancipation of their workforce. At first, they tried to keep the places running on free workers, but found the restrictions imposed by the Freedman's Bureau to be unendurable. Then they began convict-leasing and found that that answered better. Throughout the 1870s, things went well enough, until the great agricultural depression struck in 1880. The downturn lingered on, driving many farmers into penury. It was after a year or two of struggling on in greatly straitened circumstances that the sons of the men who had founded the farms took a hand in the matter. Dave Tanner and his good friend Jack Lawrence were both at that time a year or two short of their thirtieth birthdays. They were sharp, vicious and utterly ruthless, taking after their fathers. The only thing that stopped the pair of them turning bad and going off on the scout, however, was the fact that they could see there was still money to be made out of the land on which they had been raised.

It had been a chance discovery which had restored the fortunes of the Tanners and Lawrences, setting them on the path that would lead to their becoming the wealthiest families in Lumpkin County. During the great Georgia Gold Rush of 1829, a mine had been excavated up on Dead Man's Bluff, right in the heart of their land. For six or nine months it had provided a certain quantity of gold, before the reef vanished inaccessibly into the heart of the bluff. The amount of work entailed in following it down into the bowels of the earth would not have made the continued exploitation of the shaft an economic prospect for just the two men who were digging up at the mine and so the workings were abandoned.

Early in 1881 Dave Tanner went up to the bluff to examine the old mine workings. It was a forlorn enough hope, but financial matters were so pressing upon the families now that even a faint hope was worth exploring. With the aid of a storm lantern, Tanner examined the deepest part of the shaft that had been sunk and saw how the gold-bearing ore vanished into hard rock, where even explosives would be no use. One blast alone would be sufficient to collapse the whole mine, burying any profit beneath hundreds of tons of rock. And yet, there was no reason why a team of men working patiently with hammers and chisels could not follow the reef down into the rocks beneath the bluff. The only problem was that the wages of such a workforce would eat up any profit to be made from the gold itself; the seam that had been worked was not a brilliantly productive one, even to begin with.

It was while toying all this over in his mind that Tanner came up with the first inklings of a scheme. At first, he thrust it away. Surely it could never work? However, the more he considered the matter, the fewer problems presented themselves. There was nothing that couldn't be overcome, at least not by a ruthless and determined man such as himself. One morning, towards the end of February 1881, he talked over the matter with Jack Lawrence. There was no need to dress it all up in fine language; he and Jack knew each other well enough. Dave Tanner said to his friend, 'We all did well enough when we had slaves working the land here, wouldn't you say?'

'Better than we are doing now with free workers, that's for sure,' replied Jack Lawrence. 'Lazy scum who down tools the second your back's turned.'

'So you'd not be against bringing back the old days?'

'You say what? You must be crazy! Try and keep a bunch o' darkies under lock and key to work as field hands? Why, you'd have the Freedman's Bureau or whatever they call 'emselves these days down on you like a duck on a June bug.'

'I wasn't thinking of using black workers at all,' said Dave Tanner, 'I had in mind Mexicans.'

Briefly, Tanner outlined a plan to his childhood friend. They would use an agent to recruit young Mexican boys from poor families. Offer to apprentice them to various professions in the United States. The parents would be pleased, because it would be one less mouth to feed and they would be giving their sons a chance of a better life than they could ever dream of. Once the 14- or 15-year-olds landed in a country where they didn't speak the language, they could be transported up to Dead Man's Bluff and set to work for just the cost of their food. As Tanner put it, 'Hell, we can feed 'em mostly on black-eyed beans. It'll cost next to nothing.'

Lawrence rubbed his chin meditatively and said, 'We'd need somebody to watch over them and make sure they worked hard.'

'Ain't we got Thumper O'Shea? Best damned overseer in the county till those cursed Yankees freed all the darkies. He'd take the job, for a bet.'

So it was that the scheme was hatched which would bring back slavery to a small corner of the state of Georgia. There were the most ferocious legal penalties for keeping men as slaves, up to and including hanging. If they were detected in the act then Dave Tanner and Jack Lawrence would most likely forfeit their lives, but then again, they didn't plan on being caught.

Scraping together the seed money necessary to launch this new venture was not easy and in fact entailed mortgaging the very land on which the two families lived. The two patriarchs approved of the projected enterprise and that was all that mattered. Like their sons, they had been right sorry to see the end of slavery and welcomed an opportunity to bring it back in this way.

The first five boys arrived at Dead Man's Bluff only two months after the capital had been raised and it was immediately apparent that the whole idea was a sound one. A makeshift camp was set up outside the old workings and because there was no need to fret about what others might think, no attempt was made to deceive either the boys or the overseer as to the true nature of the enterprise. Shackles were hammered onto their ankles and they were chained to their cots at night. 'Thumper' O'Shea was obliged in the early days to live up to his sinister sobriquet; delivering a number of fierce beatings until the boys understood how the land lay. It was to be another six months, though, before he inadvertently killed one of the youths when one of his drunken assaults caused the boy to slip and crack his head on a rock.

Dave Tanner was furious when first he learned of the death of one of the boys he had imported, seeing it much as he would the wanton destruction of one of his horses. However, O'Shea assured him that the others were working a good deal harder now, terrified that the same fate might befall them also. After the first year or two, deaths among the workers became so common as to no longer to be particularly worthy of remark. Conditions at the camp were not conducive to good health; the poor diet, combined with gruelling hours of working underground, added to its toll. No doctor could, of course, be called to treat either illness or injury and so a minor wound, when once it became infected could lead to gangrene and death.

The high turnover of workers at Dead Man's Bluff was a constant source of irritation to Tanner and Lawrence, because of the extra expense and increased risk of regularly finding replacements for those who died. Each death led to friction with 'Thumper' O'Shea and the other three men who tended the slaves up at the bluff, but there was no question of getting rid of either O'Shea or the others. They all knew too much about the business and if any of them was to find himself in jeopardy from the law, then he would certainly try to strike a bargain by betraying his employers.

One thing was beyond all question and that was that the mine was now yielding enough gold to make the farming taking place on the plain below the bluff almost irrelevant. There was no doubt at all that the slaves had served to make the gold mine a glorious success.

CHAPTER 6

The four robbers proceeded at a steady trot along the track, leaving cattle prints in their wake. It was torture not being able to gallop at top speed, but the gait of a galloping horse leaving vastly different tracks from that of a patiently plodding steer would have raised the liveliest suspicions among anybody who was tracking them.

Eventually, Pat Seldon judged that it was safe to stop and remove the leather stockings that their horses had been wearing. When once this was done, the four of them galloped off in the opposite direction to Atlanta, just as fast as they were able. It was not for an hour or more that they slowed down to a trot, having alternated cantering and galloping until the beasts they were riding were glistening with sweat and their mouths dripping with white foam.

At length, Seldon said, 'Whoa, now. Let's set a while and see where we are.' All four of them reined in and waited to hear what their leader had to say.

'First off, is where I want to know what you been up to,' said Seldon, turning to the half breed. 'You're all over blood and whatever you done, we all like to be suspicioned for. What happened at Booker's house?'

Jimmy Two Fists shrugged indifferently, saying, 'Don't see as it matters now.'

'Don't you take that line with me, boy. I asked you a straight question. How'd you get so spattered and besmeared with blood. You hurt somebody?'

'You might say so,' replied the breed. 'Then what? Less you're some powerful magic man, you ain't about to raise the dead back to life.'

'Dead?' exclaimed Seldon in horror. 'You mean to say you killed one o' them in the house?'

'Killed the whole boilin' of 'em,' announced Jimmy Two Fists, casually. 'Servants too.'

Even such a hardened wretch as Seldon, who a few hours earlier had himself killed a harmless and inoffensive old woman, was appalled at hearing of such a slaughter. 'Not the children? Tell me you spared them?'

'Not a bit of it,' said the breed. 'That Booker fellow's wife said something I ain't about to take these days, touching on my own ancestry. First I killed her. Then one o' the other women tried to flee, so I killed her too. Then, you believe it or not, t'other woman, the cook, she ups and goes for me with a pair o' scissors as she snatches up. So I killed her as well.'

'But the little ones,' said Seldon, 'what of them?'

'Hell, you don't reckon as I was goin' to leave

witnesses? Not after killin' those three women, I wasn't. No, they had to go too.'

It was touching to see, in a way, because although he was as hard as nails and as tough as all get out and push, Pat Seldon had a soft spot for children. The news that three little girls, the oldest of them no more than nine years of age, had been murdered in cold blood left him feeling shocked and even a little numb. Fortunately, he did not have long to reflect upon the tragedy, for as he stared in disgust at the man who had committed this dreadful crime, he heard a sharp crack and felt a heavy blow to the back of his head. There was a second bang and this time the blow struck him on his back and he found himself tumbling helplessly from his horse.

Jimmy Two Fists watched Felton Tanner shoot Seldon from behind and could not make any sense of the thing. He was still puzzling the matter over a fraction of a second later, when he was in turn shot dead by Charles Lawrence; he fired three times at the half breed, hitting him twice in the trunk and once through the head.

Once the echoes had died down and the smoke had cleared a little, Tanner said, 'Well, that went better than I expected. I would've thought Seldon might have guessed something was afoot.'

'Not he,' said Charles Lawrence. 'He didn't know a damned thing, right up 'til he died.'

The two of them dismounted and began transferring the gold from Seldon and the breed's saddle-bags to their own. It would need to be weighed and assayed, of course, but at a rough guess, there was better than twelve thousand dollars worth of bullion in their possession. Once Tanner and Lawrence had picked up with Pat Seldon and learned what he planned, they had played it low about how well they already knew each other, representing themselves as casual acquaintances. It had all gone as smooth as silk. Even if some posse should come this far, they'd have a pretty riddle to read now, with the two corpses lying here. In any case, that poor fool they had set up the day before would perhaps take the whole thing upon his own shoulders. He would be lynched or maybe legally hanged and there would be an end to the matter. There never was a sweeter scheme.

After he had parted from the strange fellow who had sold him such a beautiful mare, complete with tack, for the paltry sum of ten dollars Ezekiel Cartwright decided that he was in no especial hurry to return to Atlanta. While he was out in the open country with his new mount, he thought that he might as well get the measure of her and put her through her paces. So it was that he began fooling around; trying out a little dressage. The mare was responsive to his slightest command, needing only the merest pressure from his knees to divine what he wished. Then Cartwright thought that he'd see how swift the creature was. He decided to race her along what he thought be a mile; the distance between two lightning-struck trees standing beside the track. As he began this little test of his new horse's stamina and speed, Cartwright saw that a body of riders were heading his way from the direction of Atlanta. He thought no more about this and proceeded to try to time the mare over a mile, counting out loud, slowly and carefully, 'One crocodile, two crocodile, three crocodile ...' as he rode.

By the time he started this little game, Cartwright saw that the riders were barely a quarter mile away and considered whether he should yield them the road and let them pass him before he began. Then he thought, 'What the hell, I got as much right to the highway as them.' He spurred on his horse and sped down the road, with a dozen men moving up behind him.

It never occurred to Ezekiel Cartwright for a moment that those men, who were heading out from Atlanta, could have any business with him. It wasn't until he heard the crack of a rifle that he first had a suspicion that something exceedingly odd was about to befall him. At first, he was minded to keep riding, but then, why should he flee from these men and who the Devil did they think they were to fire at him? Cartwright reined in and then turned his horse to face the grim-faced men who were bearing down on him.

When they reached Cartwright, some of the men went past him to cut off any attempt of his to ride off and the others took up positions around him. 'Somebody mind telling me what's going on?' asked Cartwright. 'Who shot at me just now?'

'I fired,' said a tough-looking man of fifty or so, 'but I wasn't shooting at you. Had I done so, you'd be dead. I was warning you.'

'Warning me? I don't rightly understand. What's going on here?'

'What's going on,' said a man who rode forward a little to confront Cartwright, 'is that we're after some beasts who killed a bunch of women and children. Robbed a bank too, but that's the least of it.'

Ezekiel Cartwright saw at once that the latest man to speak was sporting a silver star on his jacket. So these men, he realized, were official law and not just a gang of bandits or vigilantes. He said, a little more politely, 'I'm real sorry to hear about all that, but I still don't see what business you have with me.'

'Take out that piece o' your'n and let it drop in the road,' said the man who Cartwright took to be a sheriff or marshal, 'then get down from your horse.'

'You say what?'

There were half a dozen sharp, metallic clicks as men cocked their weapons. Cartwright knew that he was in danger of losing his life in the next few seconds if he didn't do as he was bid; and that right quick. The look in these men's eyes was deadly and he sensed that it would not take much on his part to set in train actions which would cost him his life. Very slowly, he pulled the pistol from where it hung at his hip and let it drop in the dust. Then he dismounted.

There was a strangely vulnerable feeling about

being deprived of both his horse and his gun and Cartwright hoped that it would not take long to clear up this foolishness. As he stood there, two men from the posse dismounted also and began to examine his horse. One of them lifted each hoof in turn; examining them carefully. The other began rifling through the saddle-bag at back of the saddle. The one who had been looking at the hoofs announced triumphantly, 'This is the one! Nail missing and a deep gouge, right 'cross the shoe.' If possible, the riders looked with even harder and more unpleasant eyes at Cartwright upon hearing this.

A second later came a cry from the man who had been delving in the saddle-bag. This man brought out a sheaf of papers, which were covered with various official-looking seals and stamps. The sheriff, or whoever he was, said, 'Let me have a look at them papers, Bob.' After examining them for a few seconds, he looked up and stared with loathing at Ezekiel Cartwright, saying, 'These here are bonds that were being kept in the bank vault. What have you to say about that?'

Before Cartwright had a chance to frame any reply, the man addressed as 'Bob' swung a meaty fist straight into the middle of his face, knocking him to the dirt. 'You bastard!' he said, 'I knew Jenny Booker and those little girls of hers.' He kicked Cartwright painfully in the ribs.

'That'll do,' said the sheriff, 'we ain't a goin' to beat him to death.'

'You're damned right, Sheriff,' said another member of the posse. 'What say we hang him right from that tree there?'

'Nothing o' the sort. We're taking this boy back to Atlanta. He'll stand trial for what he done. There'll be no lynching.'

There were murmurs of discontent at this and one of the riders said, 'Begging your pardon, Sheriff Baker, this son of a bitch and his partners killed four women and three little girls. There ain't need for no trial. I say as we should hang him here and now.'

Ezekiel Cartwright had been stunned by the blow to his face and then winded by the kick, but on hearing all this about the murder of women and children he knew that a terrible misunderstanding had taken place and that if he only said a few words, then he might be able to clear it all up. He struggled to his feet and said stoutly, 'This is all a heap of foolishness. I ain't killed anybody, not no how. Who says I done such a thing?'

Sheriff Baker gazed down at Cartwright and said, 'We tracked that horse o' your'n all the way from town. There's no mistaking that shoe of hers with the missing nail. And how d'you account for these bonds that was found in your saddle-bag? Then again, you was flying from us. That ain't the action of a man with nothin' to hide.'

'Flying from you? You mean galloping to yonder tree? I was tryin' out a new horse. I just bought this mare, not an hour since.'

There were mirthless chuckles at this claim, with a few of the riders shaking their heads in disbelief that anybody could take them for such fools as to swallow a parcel of lies like this. Then the man who had handed Sheriff Baker the documents from the saddle-bag gave a shout of triumph. He had unbuckled a side pocket and produced from within it a handful of gold nuggets. The sheriff cocked his head and stared at Cartwright. 'Care to explain that?'

'Like I said, I bought this mare only today. I didn't know what was stowed away in that there bag.'

'What?' said another of the men. 'You bought horse and tack together? That's an unusual circumstance, wouldn't you say?'

Cartwright felt as though the coils of some monstrous beast were tightening around him; preparing to crush him to death. He hardly knew what to say and those watching him took his indecision and silence for guilt. Sheriff Baker said, 'I heard enough. Bob, you bind his hands and set him on that horse of his. We're going back to town and he'll lodge in my gaol this night.'

'And that's how it was,' said Cartwright. 'I was a prisoner for the next forty years, 'til yesterday in fact.' The recitation of his tale had exhausted him. It had been many years since he had spoken at such length and the experience was not a pleasant one for him.

'So you never even knew Tanner or any of the

others?' asked Enoch Blake. 'You just met them in Atlanta, as you walked down the street?'

'That's the strength of it. I don't ask you to believe me, mind. Couldn't care less, if you want the truth.'

'I have a record of that trial, by which I mean your trial, somewhere in one of these volumes,' said Blake, waving his hand to indicate the leather-bound books that encompassed them on three sides of the room. 'Mind if I reach it down now?'

'It's nothing to me. I'll be going directly, so you can look at any of your books you've a mind to.'

'I never knew such a hasty man as you, Cartwright. Here I am, ready to believe your story and offer my support and yet you can't wait to get away.'

'I didn't ask for your support, Blake. Don't need it. And if you think that you're doing me some big favour by believing what I say, well then you're wrong on that count as well.'

It seemed to Enoch Blake that it was time to lay down all his cards and see how his guest would take it. He said, 'Here's the way of it. I was a sheriff myself for thirty years. I've been farming since then and now I reckon I could do with a spell in harness as a lawman again, or something like. I'm offering to aid you in what you are doing.'

Cartwright thought that it would be ungracious to snub such an advance and said simply, 'I don't need any man's help. I'm grateful for the offer, but what I'm about needs only me to accomplish it.'

'You wouldn't like to set the record straight? Have folk know that you were innocent of all those deaths?'

It was plain that the man sitting opposite him had not thought of the matter in those terms, having only been concerned with speaking man to man with Felton Tanner. He hesitated for a while, finally saying, 'I don't see how that would be possible. Not after all these years.'

'Will you let me try? We can go through the record of the trial together and see if anything was missed. Then, if you're willing, I'll come up to Fort Crane with you. I know the sheriff there. Professionally, that is. I could maybe help to set up a meeting between you and Felton Tanner. What d'you say?'

It was plain that Cartwright was considering the idea carefully. He was not in the habit of accepting help from anybody and so it was not to be expected that he would jump at Blake's proposition. At length, he smiled; the first real sign of human emotion that the retired sheriff had yet seen on the fellow's face. Cartwright said, 'You can be mighty persuasive, Blake. If you want to tag along of me and maybe break the monotony of your farming a bit into the bargain, I won't say no. Long as it's understood, plain as plain, that I'll do as I wish and neither you nor any living man will stop me.'

'I wouldn't try and get in your way. I've an idea that it might end badly for one or the other of us. If I can lend a hand to you, then I will. As long as this truly ain't about wreaking revenge nor nothing at all tending in that direction?'

'Revenge!' snorted Cartwright. 'I can't get back those lost forty years and killing Tanner wouldn't help me none. I just want to speak to him and see if he isn't a bit ashamed of what he did all those years ago. There's nothing more to the case than that.'

'Well in that case, I'll see if that daughter of mine might be induced to brew us up a fresh pot of coffee and we'll talk over how best to go about this. And Cartwright, I thank you again for your coming to that child's aid and rescuing her like you did. I can never repay you.'

Ezekiel Cartwright shrugged and remarked, 'Any real man would have done as much.'

CHAPTER 7

Dave Tanner was going over some paperwork with his friend and business partner. Although they were doing better than ever out of the mine up on Dead Man's Bluff, there were still one or two matters that disturbed him. He said, 'How many boys've we lost in the last year, would you say? Six, seven?' By 'lost', he meant, of course, 'died'.

'Something like that,' replied Lawrence indifferently. 'Why d'you ask?'

''Cause it's getting to be a regular damned nuisance, having to arrange for replacements. I don't think O'Shea's taking as good care of them as he might. Either that or one or two of those other roughnecks he has helping him make too free with their fists and boots.'

At this, Jack Lawrence laughed out loud. 'You kill me sometimes, man, you really do,' he declared. 'Course he ain't taking good care of 'em. Not if you mean feeding 'em on turtle soup and venison and then tucking them up under eiderdown quilts at bedtime, he ain't. We pay him to get as much work out of those lazy greasers as ever he may. He's a whale at that, all right.'

'Yeah, that's true enough. Only thing is, I don't want to start bringing in more than one or two consignments a year. Every time we land a cargo at New Orleans, that's one more risk.'

It was indicative of their attitude to the children that they acquired in this way that both Tanner and Lawrence referred to them habitually as 'cargo'. It was a way of blinding themselves to the fact that they were really trading in human lives. Perhaps for the same reason, neither of them visited the workings very frequently and when they did, they tried not to see the boys themselves, conducting all their business with 'Thumper' O'Shea or one of his lieutenants.

'There's another thing,' said Tanner, 'O'Shea's getting greedier than ever lately. He's a way of talking sometimes, makes it almost sound like he's a threatening me.'

His friend shrugged. 'O'Shea'd hang same as us if all that goes on up on the bluff came to light. He's not a fool; he knows that as well as we do. So do those others. We're all bound to each other, as you might say.'

'Happen so,' said Tanner, 'but he's still eating into the profits.'

'You want we should go and speak to him together?'

'Yeah. What say this afternoon?'

'Sounds good.'

It was at this point that Tanner's father entered the room. He had just recently celebrated his eighty-third birthday, but he was as sprightly and full of vim as he had been a decade earlier. 'The Devil looks after his own!' was how some of the townsfolk in Fort Crane set out the case. Felton Tanner looked to be in an irritable mood and he waved Jack Lawrence back into his seat when the younger man made to rise as a mark of respect. 'You're a rare set of scoundrels,' was the old man's greeting. 'Not going to mention Zeke Cartwright being set loose, hey? What d'you mean by it?'

Dave Tanner had taken care to conceal the newspaper containing the news of Cartwright's release; an artifice which had evidently failed. He was at a loss to know how to answer his father, so Jack Lawrence cut in smoothly, saying, 'I'm to blame, sir. We didn't want to distress you none.'

Felton Tanner was anything but appeased by this answer. 'You'd do better to mind your own damned business,' he asserted warmly. 'You always were a sight too keen on poking that nose of yours into other people's affairs. Either of you think I care a tinker's cuss if that lily-livered little shrimp's been let free now? Huh! He was nobody then and I doubt forty years in the pen's changed him aught.' Catching sight of the papers and account books which his son had been examining, the old man said, 'Those the figures for the mine? Hand 'em over.'

Dave Tanner and Jack Lawrence might have been

a tough enough pair in the world at large, but in the presence of old Mr Tanner, they were as meek as lambs. Besides which, all the land, including the bluff, belonged in reality to the old man and his former partner. Dave Tanner stood up and passed the books across to where his father stood waiting. Without thanking his son, old man Tanner took everything across to a nearby table and stood there, totting up the columns of figures effortlessly in his head.

'What's this?' Felton Tanner asked. 'This amount, fifty-nine dollars for premiums. What are premiums?'

'It's money we collected from the boys' parents, Pa. You know, it's the thing for apprentices to pay a sum to be allowed to start learning a trade? They call that the premium. Those boys' families would be right suspicious if we didn't demand something, so we take five or ten dollars, as they can afford, and make out we're doing them a favour by lettin' 'em in so cheap.'

The old man gave a long, wheezing laugh of amusement, saying when he'd finished chuckling, 'Oh, that's rich! You charge them to send their sons into slavery. That's very good. Well done, the two of you.'

After his father had left, Dave Tanner said, 'The old fellow's still as sharp as a lancet.'

'More than can be said for my pa,' said Lawrence, a little wistfully. 'He's in his dotage. Don't even know where he is these days, not half the time.'

Two hours after the conversation with Felton Tanner, his son set off for Dead Man's Bluff. He and

Jack Lawrence rode at a steady trot; neither of them being in any hurry to reach their destination. Although they were perfectly familiar with the conditions in the camp attached to the mine, they neither of them liked seeing the place. As long as they did not go too frequently to the bluff, both men were able to persuade themselves that the place was not quite as dreadful as all that. The reality was always something worse than their memories.

After negotiating the steep path winding up the side of the bluff, they opened the gate in the barbed wire fence and let themselves into the camp. The area occupied by the mine and living quarters was a deep hollow, surrounded by soaring, sheer walls of blank rock cliff. It would take an agile and determined man to scale those lofty heights. The area thus environed by the rocks was roughly five acres or so. The workers – both Tanner and Lawrence maintained the mental fiction that these men were workers and not slaves – lived in old army tents that had been bought cheaply from a nearby base. They were leaky and draughty and in the winter there was a lot of sickness from the cold and damp.

There was something unhealthy and malign about the mining camp, which made both Dave Tanner and Jack Lawrence reluctant to visit too often, notwithstanding the fact that it had been they themselves who had set it up in the first place. They were happy now, though, to live on the profits and do their best to forget the actual source of their prosperity. Tanner said, shivering, 'This place surely gives me the creeps!'

'I know what you mean. Still, I'd sooner these greasers were suffering than me and my family. You recollect how tough things were getting when that damned depression first began to bite.'

'Sure. I guess I just don't want to see it.'

Lawrence laughed and said, 'Why, you got the makings of a soul there! You feeling guilty?'

For a moment, Dave Tanner felt inclined to be tetchy, but then he shrugged and said, 'No, just let's us be out of this place as soon as might be.'

The railroad line to Atlanta passed only a mile from Enoch Blake's house. He and Zeke Cartwright were up early to catch the train at a little way-halt which lay just beyond the boundary of Blake's fields. Catherine made breakfast for the two men, who needed to be off no later than six if they were to be sure of catching the train to the city. Cartwright felt the girl's eyes on him as he ate and it made him feel a mite uncomfortable. When they were leaving the house, Catherine Blake came up to him suddenly and, with no warning, kissed him on the cheek. Without saying a word, she turned and went back into the house.

Enoch Blake watched this proceeding with amusement and said, 'You got a friend there at any rate, Cartwright.' The other man grunted.

The journey to Atlanta took only a half hour when once they had caught the train. Before they alighted,

Blake said, 'I don't suppose you'd care to hand over those pistols to me? It makes me kind of nervous, like you might forget yourself if we should end up meeting with this Felton Tanner.'

Cartwright laughed shortly and said, 'No, I don't believe I'll be parted from them. Feels good to be a free man with a gun in my belt.'

'They make you look like a real desperado, you know.'

'You think I care? I'm like to be dead in a few months.'

There was a connecting train leaving for Fort Crane almost immediately. Zeke Cartwright wasn't sorry that they had no time to spend in Atlanta; the place would have been unbearably haunted for him as the last town where he'd spent a free day in forty years. They were only ten minutes in the depot before the train for Fort Crane departed.

So used were Tanner and Lawrence to visiting the mine and camp from time to time to keep an eye on things, that neither of them had the least apprehension that things could ever go wrong. The boys there, none of whom was above sixteen or seventeen years of age, all had a hangdog air and walked about slowly and sullenly; like they had long ago given up all hope. This was in addition to the fact that all wore shackles on their ankles. So it was that as they stood chatting to Thumper O'Shea on that particular afternoon, nobody had the least premonition of disaster. Two of the other men who operated the mine and oversaw the workforce had gone into town for supplies, leaving only O'Shea and a fellow called Thompson to keep things going.

There were currently seventeen youths at the camp and they worked in shifts; half down in the mine at any one time, while those on the surface worked to move the spoil that had been excavated and carry out such work as fetching water. The boys spoke only Spanish, which neither O'Shea nor any of the other men supervising them had ever bothered to master. A natural consequence of this was that none of the overseers ever had the least idea of what was being talked about by the boys. The first sign that anything might be amiss came when one of the boys stumbled and fell while he was carrying a basket of stones which had just been brought to the surface. He fell heavily and did not rise, but lay quite still.

'Shit,' said Jack Lawrence, 'what's happened there?'

'Ah, leave him be,' said O'Shea in an unconcerned voice. 'The idle bastard's probably just snatching a few minutes' rest.'

'Yes,' said Tanner, 'and that's just like you, O'Shea. Those boys are valuable to us. You wouldn't let a horse go lame, careless like that, would you? I'm telling you, those boys cost us a sight more than horses. Just get over and see what's wrong with him.'

Thumper O'Shea did not really care to be spoken to in this way, even by the men who paid his wages. He was worried that some of the boys might have heard and that would never do. It would lower him in their estimation. Undermining his authority might make them disposed to be idle or rebellious. He said, 'Listen, Mr Tanner, you got no complaint 'bout the amount o' work I get out of those boys. You'd go a long way to find anybody could run this place better than me.'

Sensing that it was time to smooth things over a little, Jack Lawrence said, 'Ah, we're not complaining, man. But really, I think that young fellow's hurt. Look, he still ain't moved.'

'If it'll ease your mind, I'll tend to him. You want I should send to town for the doctor?' asked O'Shea facetiously. 'I'm sure he'd be right glad to come up here and look after the boys.' Having delivered himself of this witticism, O'Shea stomped over to where the boy who had tripped up still lay face down on the ground.

When he reached the youngster, Thumper O'Shea prodded him in the ribs with his boot, saying roughly, 'Get up, you lazy young devil.' There was no response. It struck O'Shea that there might genuinely be something the matter with the boy and he felt annoyed that this had happened when the two bosses were in the camp. He crouched down and lifted the fellow's head by the simple expedient of grabbing a handful of his hair. The boy's eyes didn't so much as flicker.

Just as O'Shea was convinced that the young Mexican really was badly injured, the boy twisted round, as lithe as a cat, and produced from somewhere a rusty spike, which was about six inches in length. This he drove as hard as he could into Thumper O'Shea's face; ripping through his right cheek and splitting his eyeball in half. The overseer gave an agonized scream and clutched at his wounded face.

Both Dave Tanner and Jack Lawrence stood rooted to the spot, quite unable to comprehend what they were seeing. O'Shea lurched to his feet and staggered away from the youth who had been lying prone. The young Mexican at once leapt up and ran across to the tents; the chain connecting his ankles causing him to make short, mincing steps, which would under other circumstances have been somewhat comical. Neither Tanner nor Lawrence, though, felt in the least inclined to laugh just then. It took them a few moments to collect themselves and when they did, both drew their pistols and looked warily towards the tents, where the boy who had attacked O'Shea had now vanished. Not a sound came from that direction and it was hard to know what to do for the best. Thumper O'Shea had collapsed to his knees about twenty yards from them and was making mewling noises suggestive of great pain and suffering. Like so many bullies, he was excessively concerned about his own skin and being attacked and injured in that way had come as a terrible shock to him.

The train to Fort Crane was smaller and less comfortably appointed than the one which had taken Cartwright and Blake to Atlanta. Not many folk of importance lived out towards the North Georgia Mountains and maybe the railroad company didn't feel that there was any great purpose in lavishing luxurious fittings and soft seats upon the farmers and merchants who did travel that route. Once they were settled into their seats and the train was fairly on its way, Blake said, 'I worked with Sheriff Isaacs for quite some time. You'd put me in an awkward position were anything untoward to happen in Fort Crane.'

'Am I supposed to worry about your standing with some fellow I never set eyes on in my life?' asked Cartwright, a glint of amusement in his eyes. 'You're the one who was so keen to tag along here, Blake. I didn't twist your arm.'

'You're a right difficult man to get along with, Cartwright, you know that?'

'When a man's had everything took from him and he's about to lose his life into the bargain, maybe he don't have time for social graces.'

Cartwright stared out of the window for a spell and then said, 'I won't embarrass you with your friend, you needn't fret. You seem a decent enough type and I wouldn't put you in a false position.'

'What will you say to Felton Tanner, always allowing that he'll speak to you?'

There was silence for a while before Cartwright answered. Blake wondered if he was going to tell him to mind his own business, but eventually the other man spoke. He said, 'You want the truth, you can have it. I found the Lord in gaol. Yes, I know what you're thinking; a lot of those villains in the penitentiary start sucking up to the preachers and pretending to be pious. I'd no need to do that; there wasn't much good it would've done me.'

'I'm a church-going man myself,' ventured Blake, 'I guessed you were of that mould.'

Cartwright looked as though the effort of talking so much was tiring him a little, for there was a sheen of sweat on his forehead. Blake said gently, 'If you don't feel up to talking, then just tell me to shut up and keep quiet.'

'It's not my illness. I'm just not used to saying much about my own self. Anyways, you want to know what I want from Tanner. It's easy enough. I want to get right with everybody before I meet my maker. I'll give Felton Tanner the chance to say that he's sorry for what he did. Whether he does or doesn't, I want him to know that I forgive him. I wouldn't want to leave this world holding a grudge against any man.'

For a moment, Blake felt as though the breath had been knocked from his body, so unexpected was what the grim-looking man sitting opposite him had said. Then he shook his head slowly, saying, 'Well, I never reckoned ever to meet a real live saint. But I guess you're about as close to it as I'll ever come. You've spent forty years in gaol, you're dying and all that's on your mind is to find the man who did this to you, so that you can forgive him? If that don't beat all!'

'I'm no saint, Blake. I just wouldn't have the man who wronged me go to his grave without having a chance to repent. For the sake of his own soul, you know.'

After having spoken so much, Cartwright seemed to be tired and so the two men sat there without saying anything further. After a little while, Cartwright drifted off to sleep and the former sheriff watched him as his chest rose and fell. Enoch Blake had come across many preachers, missionaries and priests in his time, but none of them had ever impressed him as powerfully as this man. Rough and ready as he seemed to be, Ezekiel Cartwright was like some Old Testament prophet. He tried to think how he might himself feel, if he had been unjustly locked up for all those years and thirty of them in solitary confinement. It didn't bear thinking about. Yet no sooner had the man been released from prison, than he had made a beeline towards the one who had condemned him to that living hell, with the sole motive of forgiveness in his heart. Why, it was a regular miracle!

Blake closed his eyes as well and the rocking of the train lulled him too into a state of profound relaxation. Pretty soon, the two elderly men were both slumbering as the train hurtled towards Fort Crane.

CHAPTER 8

'Where's that other damned guy,' asked Dave Tanner, 'the one who's supposed to be here with O'Shea?'

There was an eerie silence around the camp and neither Tanner nor Lawrence quite knew what to do next. Thumper O'Shea was rocking to and fro a few yards away, moaning and keening to himself, but that was the only sound that could be heard. When the attack came, it took them altogether by surprise.

Eight young men came charging from the entrance of the mine; all brandishing picks, crowbars and spades. For a second, Tanner was too taken aback to do anything, then he realized that their lives were hanging by a thread. He fired at the leading figure in the rush, a tall, slender, copper-skinned youth who looked as though he was at least half Indian. The spell was broken and Jack Lawrence too began firing, taking down two of the others. The charge faltered and then the remaining five boys backed off and scuttled towards the tents. It was at this point that the other two overseers returned from their expedition, bursting onto the scene with their guns at the ready, having heard the shooting as they unlocked the gate leading into the compound.

'Where the hell you boys been?' growled Jack Lawrence. 'We could o' been killed here, for all you men cared about it.'

'Thumper asked us to go over to Fort Crane for provisions,' said one of the men indignantly. 'He's the boss.'

'No,' said Lawrence angrily, '*I'm* the boss. Me and Mr Tanner here. While you clowns have been gallivanting off the Lord knows where, there's been a rising here.'

'A rising?' said the other man. 'Why, I don't rightly understand you.'

Without taking his eyes off the cluster of tents, where his erstwhile adversaries were now hiding, Tanner said, 'It's simple enough. O'Shea's been injured and those men have gone for us. Where's the other one of you fellows?'

'Sam? He stayed here with Thumper, I mean Mr O'Shea.'

'Either of you two speak Spanish?' asked Tanner. 'We need to parlay with those savages.'

The two foremen looked at each other blankly. A mastery of foreign languages had never been represented to them as being one of the qualifications needed for their work. As they had understood it, the job entailed only forcing half-starved peasants to work until they were at the point of death from sheer exhaustion and, when necessary, encouraging them with curses and blows. Nobody had ever suggested that they needed any talents or skills other than these.

'Never mind,' said Dave Tanner, 'we have to restore order. We just killed three of them. There's seventeen altogether, that right?'

'Sure,' agreed one of the overseers. 'Leaves us with....' He tried and failed to subtract three from seventeen in his head, without the aid of his fingers. Ciphering, like the study of Spanish, was another of those arcane skills that he had not yet been called upon to exercise since taking up his post at Dead Man's Bluff.

'You men are about as much use as ...' began Lawrence, but then ground to a halt, unable to find a simile which sufficiently expressed his low opinion of the capabilities of the two men whose job it was to enforce order at the mine. He continued, 'We got to get those men to understand that capers like this won't answer. We lost three of them, another'll make no odds.'

Tanner at once caught his old friend's drift, saying, 'You mean the one who wounded O'Shea?'

'That I do,' said Lawrence grimly. 'We don't show them once for all who's in charge, then next time we come up here, we'll find they've all broken out.'

Turning to the two overseers who had lately returned from Fort Crane, Jack Lawrence said, 'Those men in the tents have only picks and spades. We've four guns between us.' A thought struck him and he said, 'Either o' you boys have a sawn-off scattergun near at hand?'

It appeared that such an article was not to be found and Lawrence made a mental note that after the day's events, it would be necessary to strengthen the armament of the camp and ensure that none of those whose job it was to supervise those men ever took any more chances.

Both Dave Tanner and Jack Lawrence were, in the usual way of things, resolute men who were swift to take action. Their vacillation in the present situation stemmed not from a want of courage or weakness of will, but solely from the fact that in seven years there had never been any trouble of this kind. It was altogether unheard of and such a novel state of affairs had thrown both of the men quite out of kilter.

After a brief, whispered consultation, out of earshot of the two overseers, Tanner and Lawrence told them the plan of campaign, which was that they would all walk slowly to the tents and then persuade the men there that if they carried on with their revolt, then they would all die. Once they had quelled the disorder, then an example would be made of the one who looked to be their leader; he who had injured Thumper O'Shea so grievously.

The four of them moved forward and found that the fourteen men in the tents were waiting, their tools clutched in their hands like weapons, but knowing that another sudden rush would bring about further deaths. They eyed the four men with guns warily. Dave Tanner soon identified the young man who had sparked off the trouble by going for O'Shea. He gestured at this man and indicated that the fellow should come forward. Although he didn't know if any of that rabble spoke or understood English, he talked quietly and reassuringly, in a tone of voice which suggested that he was more grieved than angry at the way things had turned out. He said, 'Just come forward now. Nobody means you any harm, we just want to talk.' As he said this, Tanner made beckoning gestures, waving his hands invitingly towards his own chest. 'I ain't angry 'bout this. Neither are any of these other men. We just got to sort matters out and find out what's to do next, you understand me?'

When the fellow who had ripped open O'Shea's face with a chunk of rusty metal was clear of the other workers, standing proudly and quite without fear, about fifteen feet from the Americans, Tanner raised his pistol and deliberately shot the man twice in the chest. Then he walked up close and put a ball through the Mexican's face as well. If that didn't serve to show those greasers the cost of rebellion, then nothing would.

Felton Tanner was in a restless mood. A year or two back, he would have saddled up and ridden over to see Charlie Lawrence, but his old friend was in his dotage and such visits were painful and depressing. Half the time these days, Charlie didn't know where he was or even the year he was living in. Increasingly, when Felton did see him, the other man was tormented by the thought of the people who had died as a result of his crimes. He was also prone to talking of young Zeke Cartwright and the wrong they had done him. Odd times, it appeared to Felton Tanner that his old comrade was actually haunted by the spirits of those he had robbed and killed so many years ago. There had been many such before they took part in the great Atlanta gold robbery, but it was the victims of that crime who seemed to occupy most of Charlie Lawrence's waking hours and, for all Tanner knew to the contrary, his night time dreams as well.

For his own part, the only regrets that Felton Tanner had about the past were opportunities he had missed. There were women he wished he had seduced, men he should have killed or at the very least beaten, gullible types he might have cheated. That was the only thing approaching remorse that Felton Tanner experienced as his eighty-fourth year drew on. He had been amused to hear of that poor sap Cartwright being freed from gaol when he was in his sixties. It would have eased his mind had the fellow been hanged forty years ago, but he felt no animosity towards him; merely contempt, mingled with a profound satisfaction that another man had suffered in order to provide Tanner and his family with a comfortable life.

The worst thing about getting old, apart from the dramatic decline in his sexual ability and the length of time he could go without emptying his bladder, was the way that folks tried to sidestep you and carry on with their lives without taking your own views and opinions into the reckoning. He had noticed this disturbing trend even among members of his own family. How dare his son try and hide the newspaper from him? And Charlie's little runt, that Jack. He was another of them. Smooth and polite as you like to his face, but always up to something behind his back.

It was while the old man was stumping about the house and musing in this fashion that he heard the thunder of hoofs and saw three riders fetch up in the yard outside. Looking from the window, Felton Tanner could see that one of the men looked to be badly hurt, with his face a bloody mess. The other two riders, who were apparently caring for the wounded man, were his son and Jack Lawrence. The ghost of a smile flickered around the old man's mouth. He had a suspicion that things were about to grow mighty interesting for a change and he had a sudden premonition that for once, he would be in the thick of the action and not merely hearing about it second hand when somebody bothered to tell him what had been going on.

Ezekiel Cartwright woke first from his nap and was, for a moment, confused and disoriented to find himself on a moving vehicle. For a moment, he had thought he was back in his cell at Milledgeville. He looked across at where the retired sheriff was snoozing and wondered why he had allowed himself to become entangled in this way with another man's business. It was plain to

Cartwright that Enoch Blake was fulfilling some need of his own in setting out on this journey and that Cartwright's own requirements were only a secondary consideration. Still and all, Blake struck him as a decent and God-fearing man and there was no reason that their trails should not run side by side for a spell.

Fort Crane was neither a populous nor prosperous town. It had been founded sixty years earlier, during the Georgia Gold Rush, but had been in a state of gradual and genteel decline ever since. At its peak, some six thousand souls had lived there; now there were barely a quarter of that number. The sheriff, Albert Isaacs, was a quiet and sober man, ten years younger than Blake. He ran the town with a slack rein, only really cracking down hard on crimes of violence. It was widely known that while he might turn a blind eye to a still being operated up in the hills, let anybody lay a hand upon his wife and Sheriff Isaacs would soon be knocking on the door and setting that man on the right path.

Isaacs was surprised and pleased to see his old friend Enoch Blake walk unannounced into his office, just before midday. 'Well, as I live and breathe,' he exclaimed happily, 'Blake, you old rascal! What brings you to this neck of the woods? Pleasure and not business, I'm hopeful?'

'Ah, I ain't been to see you for the longest while, Isaacs. Thought I'd kind of drop by, you know.'

The sheriff was looking past Blake at his companion.

'Who's your friend? You goin' to introduce us?'

Cartwright, who had no time for polite manners, spoke for himself, saying, 'My name's Cartwright. Ezekiel Cartwright, although some call me Zeke.'

There was a deadly silence as Sheriff Isaacs absorbed this strange and unexpected piece of intelligence. Then he said, 'I'm guessing that there isn't more than one man of about your age bearing that name in Georgia?'

'Wouldn't have thought so, no,' replied Cartwright indifferently. 'Happen you've heard of me?'

'Happen so,' said Isaacs, staring with loathing at the man standing by the door of his office. He said to Blake, 'Would you mind favouring me with a few words? We can take a turn up the street while this man waits our pleasure out on the sidewalk.' Without even looking at Cartwright, the sheriff ushered his friend out onto the street and, still without taking any further notice of Cartwright, locked the door behind him and took Blake's arm, guiding him up the street.

'Thought you might at least offer us some coffee,' said Blake, trying to maintain a light tone. 'You always used to keep a pot on the stove for visitors.'

'What in the hell do you think you're about,' asked Isaacs, 'bringing that killer here? A woman killer, what's more. Four women and three little children. You forgotten that?'

'He didn't do it, Isaacs. You think I'd keep company with a man of that brand?

His friend snorted in derision. 'Sure, I never met

one man as had been in the pen who was guilty. What is it, you going soft in the head, living out on that farm of yours?'

Slowly, but persuasively, Enoch Blake set out the case for believing that Cartwright had suffered an appalling miscarriage of justice. The two of them walked round the town, losing track of the time for the better part of three quarters of an hour, until Sheriff Isaacs was at least willing to talk to Cartwright. The turning point came when the name of Felton Tanner was mentioned.

'Tanner?' said Sheriff Isaacs sharply. 'What has he to do with this business?'

When Blake had outlined the supposed connection that had once existed between Felton Tanner and Zeke Cartwright, the sheriff rubbed his chin thoughtfully. He said, 'So you say that old man Tanner is part of this, is that the strength of it?'

'Pretty much. Why?'

'The Tanners are big wheels around here, if you take my meaning. Rich as Croesus and more or less a law unto themselves. I know that Tanner was something of a villain in his younger days, but since he and his friend bought that spread of theirs, they've lived quietly enough. Only thing is, for the last few years, nobody seems to know how they get their money. Everybody else round here, all the farmers and so on, why they're as poor as can be through that there depression that you read of in the papers. But not the Tanners and Lawrences.'

'You think the families are involved in something crooked?'

'I know damned well they are! Only thing is, I haven't a clue what. They employ a mort of men hereabouts and some of them rough customers. But how they're becoming so rich, I don't know. You say your man wants to meet up with old Tanner? Well now, whether he's innocent or guilty, that might set a hare running, as they say. Might stir things up a little and we'll see what comes of it.'

'You mean you'll help us?'

Isaacs looked at his old friend and said, 'I don't know what your part in this game might be, Blake. I guess you've a different aim from your friend Cartwright. Well, that's fine, 'cause I got my own motives. I'll help you all right. Fact I'll ride up to Tanner's place with you and see what comes of it. It's about time that I gave those boys up there a bit of a jolt.'

When O'Shea had been helped off his horse and brought into the kitchen, Felton Tanner eyed the man with interest. His cheek had been sliced open down to the bone. His right eyeball was partly hanging from the socket, on account of whatever had been used to cut his cheek had also torn away the lower eyelid which, in the normal way of things, kept a man's eye in its rightful place. He'd seen a whole heap of gruesome injuries in his time, but nothing to approach this. He asked his son curiously, 'What caused the wound?'

Dave Tanner looked at his father in a distracted fashion, his mind wholly occupied on the terrible dangers that this episode might bring down upon his head and asked blankly, 'Caused what?'

'Yon fellow's face. What did that to him?'

'I don't know. A piece of old iron, I think. Rusty as hell. Why'd you ask?'

'No reason. I'm just curious is all.'

His son shook his head and carried on trying to tend to O'Shea, who was alternately roaring with pain and whimpering in terror like a little girl. One good thing about this mess was that there was nobody else in the house to witness it. Neither the Tanners nor the Lawrences kept servants. Both houses were exclusively masculine domains and it little mattered to any of the men whether their homes got a little dusty from time to time. Every so often, once a month or so, they hired help from the town; women who came out to clean the houses from top to bottom. Other than that, one of the hands who lived in the cabins on the edge of their fields came to cook each evening and this fellow also washed the wares that they had been using for the last day. It was a rough and ready arrangement, which might not have suited women, but served the purposes of the four men just perfectly. Neither Dave Tanner nor Jack Lawrence had ever felt any inclination towards matrimony, which was perhaps just as well. It was hard to imagine any wife, however devoted, enduring this lifestyle for long.

'Who's looking after the mine?' asked the old man suddenly. 'There's no chance of those slaves getting out I guess?'

'No,' his son replied, 'there's two men guarding them.'

'Two men? Thought you had four up there. Where's the other one?'

'Dead.'

Felton Tanner made an irritable clucking noise at the back of his throat. 'Dead? What became of him? And I hope you've not lost any of them slaves. God knows they cost us enough to bring up here from the coast.'

It was one of those occasions when Dave Tanner thought that he could cheerfully strangle his own father. At least Jack didn't have to put up with this. Although he tended to roam sometimes, Jack's father never tried to involve himself with the present-day business of the families. He said to his father, 'One of the overseers was killed today. Four of the workers are dead too.'

'You left just two men up at the bluff?' said Felton Tanner. 'That won't answer. What happens if they both fall asleep at once? You been too soft up there, boy. Too soft by half.'

Being called 'boy' at the age of thirty-eight was mighty irksome to Dave Tanner and it was only with the greatest effort that he succeeded in suppressing his irritation. He said, 'Thing is, Pa, we can't just let all the world and his dog know what we're about up at the bluff. We needs must think carefully about who we bring in to the business.'

'Do you think I'm a fool?' asked the old man wrathfully, 'I know as much of this business as you do. I'll go up there this day and deal with matters. It's plain that none of you noodles will be able to handle what's afoot.'

If Sheriff Isaacs thought that Cartwright would be grateful to hear that he was halfway inclined to give him the benefit of the doubt about the massacre in Atlanta all those years ago, then the old man was ready to set him straight.

'My friend Blake here, he says as you might not have been guilty of what you was convicted of,' said Isaacs. 'I trust him and I'll allow as there might be something in what he says.'

Ezekiel Cartwright looked at Isaacs impassively and said, 'Couldn't say I care one way or the other about your opinion. I ain't asking for you to think anything of me. It's all one.'

Having screwed himself up to be civil to the most notorious killer ever seen in the state of Georgia, the sheriff was a little put out to be snubbed in that way. He said, 'Well ain't you the charmer?'

Cartwright shrugged and said, 'Man gets as close to death as I am, Sheriff, he don't have a heap of time left for empty words. You fix up a meeting 'tween me and Felton Tanner, you'll be doing the right thing. There's no more to the case than that. It's your conscience. You right with the Lord?'

'That's my affair,' replied Sheriff Isaacs testily. 'I suppose we're sure that it really is Felton Tanner who tricked you all those years back? You'd know him again?'

'That I would.'

'Let's go in my office and check.'

Once Sheriff Isaacs opened the door and let the two men into his sanctum, he went rummaging round in a drawer of his desk, until he found what he wanted. It was a photograph of a celebration of the sixtieth anniversary of Fort Crane's founding, which had taken place three months previously. Being careful to hold his hand over the inscription below the picture, he held it out for Cartwright to inspect, saying, 'Recognize anybody?'

Without hesitation, Ezekiel Cartwright pointed to an old man in the front row of a group of citizens who were assembled beneath some kind of banner. 'That's the man. That's him who first told me his name was Stuart Bailey, but had letters addressed to Felton Tanner.'

'You seem mighty sure,' observed the sheriff. 'It's forty years if what you say is true.'

'Believe me, you spend thirty years in solitary and then another ten in ordinary confinement, you're not apt to forget the face of the man who sent you there.'

There was little that could be said to this and so Isaacs simply replaced the photograph from where he had got it. After pouring out coffee for his guests, he asked, 'Well then, when do you fellows want to go and pay Mr Tanner a visit?'

'The sooner the better,' said Cartwright. 'I don't know if Blake here's told you, but I'm not long for this world. I got to get things straight with that man before I die.'

The sheriff eyed the two pistols tucked nonchalantly in Cartwright's belt and then said flatly, 'We can go this very afternoon if you please. But I tell you straight, I'm not taking you out there while you're armed. My friend here says you got religion, which may or may not be true, but I won't gamble on it. We go to see Tanner, those guns stay here in my office.'

'That's reasonable,' said Cartwright and plucked the two weapons out, handing them across the desk to Isaacs. 'But I'll have them back when we return.'

CHAPTER 9

It was tolerably clear to Dave Tanner and Jack Lawrence that without the attention of a doctor, Thumper O'Shea was likely to die; if nothing else then from the blood poisoning or lockjaw which usually set in after a wound from rusty metal. The only thing was, of course, that there was not the slightest possibility of allowing a doctor, nor indeed anybody else, to see the man in this condition. It would invite all manner of dangerous and intrusive questions. Then again, there was the matter of how to run the mine, now that they had lost two of the men charged with overseeing the place and maintaining good order there. It was while Tanner and Lawrence were mulling over these problems, having persuaded O'Shea to lie down in another room, that Jack Lawrence happened to glance out of the window and saw Sheriff Isaacs riding along the track to the house. 'Ah no,' he muttered, 'that's all we need.'

'What's the problem?' asked Dave Tanner, before he too looked out of the window and gave voice to an even stronger expression of dismay. His father joined them and gave a short laugh. 'What are you boys fretting about?' he said, 'Albert Isaacs is an old woman. He don't know a damned thing. Just relax.'

'Who're those men with him?' wondered Lawrence, 'I don't recollect either of them.'

Suddenly, Dave Tanner had an inexplicable sensation of impending doom. He said to his father, 'Pa, why don't you go and set with Thumper? Me and Jack can handle this.'

'I'll not be ordered about in my own home. Who do you think you are?'

'Please, Pa. Somebody needs to set with O'Shea and quiet him down if he starts raving or aught. I surely don't want Isaacs to see the state of Thumper's face; he'd be certain sure to ask a heap of questions.'

'There's something in that,' said the old man, 'but watch you don't begin acting like you're running this outfit, you hear what I tell you? And we still need to get another man up to the bluff before dark.'

'Yes, yes,' said his son hastily, 'we'll talk on that after I get rid of Isaacs and the others.'

Still grumbling to himself, Felton Tanner consented to be ushered out of the kitchen and up the stairs to the next floor, where Thumper O'Shea had been placed in a guest room.

There was no sign of life when the sheriff and his companions fetched up in the yard of the Tanners' farmhouse. He called out, 'Hallo, there! Anybody around?' Just when he was starting to think that the house was deserted, Dave Tanner came out of the side door and said in a loud, cheerful voice, 'Why, Sheriff Isaacs, it surely is good to see you. What brings you out here? Nothing wrong I hope?'

'Now why should you think in terms of things being wrong, Mr Tanner?' asked Isaacs. 'You don't have a guilty conscience, I hope?' He said all this with a wide grin on his face, like he might have been joshing, but it still grated on Tanner and made him feel like telling the sheriff to get the hell off his property.

Sheriff Isaacs was looking around with friendly interest at the yard and remarked pleasantly, 'Somebody hurt himself round here, Mr Tanner?'

'What? Why are you asking?'

''Cause I see a few drops of blood in the dust there and another splashed on that rail. They're fresh, by the look of them, and the one on the rail has spread out a little and thrown off other drops. Fell from about the height of a man in a saddle, I'd say.'

'Oh yeah, one of my men cut his self with an axe. Came up here for me to patch him up. You got sharp eyes, Sheriff and that's a fact.'

'It's what I'm paid for,' said Isaacs pleasantly. 'Mind if we come inside? Got one or two questions to ask you and your pa.'

'My father ain't here, Sheriff. Gone off for a walk. Lord knows when he'll be back.'

'That's all right. I can speak to you just as well.'

Cursing inwardly and mentally consigning the sheriff to the lowest circle of Hades, Dave Tanner invited the men to dismount and step into the house. 'If you'll wait here, I'll go round and open up the front door. We can talk in the parlour.'

'Oh no, Mr Tanner. We couldn't put you to any trouble. We'll come right round and just visit with you in the kitchen, like old friends.' With an ill grace, Tanner acceded to this request. He attributed it, quite rightly, to the sheriff wishing to snoop around and see what might have been going on in a part of the house where visitors were not normally received.

By the time he realized that the sheriff and his friends would be coming into the kitchen and not going into the parlour, it was too late for Jack Lawrence to slip off. It would have looked extremely suspicious if Isaacs had seen him scuttling away, so as not to be seen. When he saw Lawrence seated at the table, Sheriff Isaacs evinced every sign of pleasure, saying, 'Mr Lawrence! Well, this is a nice surprise.'

'I only live over the way,' Lawrence reminded him.

'Can I offer you and your friends a drink?' asked Tanner. 'Water, or something a little stronger?'

For reply, Sheriff Isaacs said casually, 'Gosh, I can see traces of blood all over. That would be the man you told me had injured himself, I guess.'

'That's right,' said Dave Tanner and turned to Lawrence, saying, 'I was telling the sheriff about that clumsy devil Tim Harding, him as cut his hand with the axe. How we'd been fixing him up.'

'You're a regular Christian, Mr Tanner,' said Isaacs. 'It does my heart good to know that such men as you are still around. And you made good efforts to clean up the blood as well. Only I can see one or two spots you missed. When will your father be back?'

'I couldn't say. He stays out for a long while.'

'Well then, I guess we'd best not take up your time. Me and my friends here will call again. This here's Mr Cartwright, Ezekiel Cartwright. He wants to talk to your father about old times. No, don't trouble yourselves. We can make our own way out.'

Things were distinctly uncomfortable for the two men who had been left in charge up on Dead Man's Bluff. There was no question of getting the young men to work; they were in far too sullen and rebellious a mood for that. Before Tanner and Lawrence had left with the wounded overseer, they had helped thread the chain through the shackles of the workers which secured them all in the tents at night. This meant that the fourteen young Mexicans were trapped where they were, but it also of course meant that while they were in that position, they could not be digging in the mine.

The system at the camp had been working well for years. New boys soon became cowed and despairing, fitting in with the way of life at the camp. Nine or ten would be working, while the remainder were chained to their bunks in the tents. There had never been any sort of mutiny before and it could only be attributed to the new boys who had lately arrived there from New Orleans. The shooting of four of their number had subdued them somewhat, but it was hard to see how things could go back to normal now, after these youths had realized that rebellion was a very real and desirable possibility.

Both the men guarding the prisoners had been horrified to see the state to which those savages had reduced the man who was supposed to be supervising them in the mine itself. They had all but torn him to shreds with their picks and spades. When Tanner had come out of the mine, he had looked sick at what he had seen, but had still insisted that the two other overseers went down into the mine to see what fate awaited them if they were careless with their charges. Now, they faced a weary and uncertain afternoon and night, just sitting there, rifles cradled in their arms, preventing any further problems until their bosses came back and told them what would be happening next.

As the three of them rode away from the Tanner place, Enoch Blake said, 'Well that was a real snipe hunt. You used to be better at handling things, Isaacs.'

His friend chuckled softly. 'I got everything I wanted. Things couldn't have gone any better.'

'Only the man I wanted to see wasn't there,' remarked Ezekiel Cartwright.

'Oh he was there all right,' said the sheriff, 'or so I

read it. None of you see them cups? Those boys was as jumpy as cats. There's something very wrong there or I miss my guess. Man cut himself with an axe indeed! Did you see that rag that had been used to wipe up the blood in the kitchen? I'm telling you, somebody was bleeding like a stuck hog. Why would those scallawags let one of their men bleed all over their house like that? They'd tend to him in the yard. No siree, that was a profitable visit and no mistake!'

Both Cartwright and Blake were, for different reasons, irritated by Sheriff Isaacs' cheerful mood. Blake said, 'You told us that you'd arrange for Cartwright here to meet up with Felton Tanner. You've not forgot that, I suppose?'

'Not a bit of it,' said Isaacs jovially. 'You're free tomorrow, I reckon Cartwright? If so, we'll turn up there real early and catch them at whatever they're about. I make no doubt that old man Tanner'll be there then.'

It was Dave Tanner's father, tougher and more wicked than the younger men, who both suggested and put into execution the only thing to be done about Thumper O'Shea. After the visitors had departed, he went down to the kitchen and said, 'That fellow up there is crying out for a doctor. He's getting ready to leave here and head off to town by himself if we won't take him.'

'The hell he is,' replied his son, 'he turns up in Fort Crane and it'll all be up with us. Isaacs is already sniffing round like a blasted dog.'

'Only one thing for it then,' said the old man. 'He'll have to go.'

'Go to town, you mean?' asked Jack Lawrence. 'Why, it's not to be thought of!'

'No, you booby,' exclaimed Felton Tanner with the greatest irascibility, 'I don't mean that he should go to town. What's wrong with you boys? Don't you see anything straight?'

'I don't understand you, Pa …' began Dave Tanner.

'Don't understand me? What's to understand? O'Shea'll have to go.' Seeing the blank looks on the faces of the two younger men, Tanner continued in a humiliatingly patient way, 'We'll have to kill him. To stop word of this getting out.'

There was an awful and undeniable logic to the suggestion. If Thumper O'Shea was to be seen in Fort Crane in his present condition, then it would lead to all sorts of questions. If blood poisoning set in, as it was almost sure to, and he became delirious, there was no telling what he might reveal during his ravings. And now, from what the old man was saying, O'Shea was getting ready to leave. Then again, even if they could persuade him to stay quiet there, that damned sheriff had promised to come back the next day and there was a man whose eyes were altogether too sharp for comfort. From a purely practical point of view, O'Shea's death would solve a lot of problems. He wasn't likely to be any use to them in the future anyway, not with only one eye and all.

'I don't know, Pa,' said Dave Tanner, 'we known Thumper these many years. I can't just kill him.'

'Ah, you're soft like your mother, God rest her,' jeered the old man. 'I'll do it if you two are too lily-livered.' He went over to the closet standing against the wall in which firearms were kept.

Jack Lawrence had merely observed the exchange between his old friend and his father, not wishing to intervene from a sense of delicacy. Neither he nor Dave Tanner were in any way sentimental, but it seemed to Lawrence a fearful thing to end a man's life just because he had become a nuisance. He said to old Mr Tanner, 'Ain't there any other course we could take, sir?'

'You want to hang?' asked the old man rhetorically. 'How many of those Mexican boys have died up on the bluff? You want Sheriff Isaacs raising a posse and digging round up there? Anybody from town sets eyes on that camp and you're both like to be lynched, never mind being arrested and brought to trial. Either way, your lives'll be worth no more than that.' He snapped his fingers to indicate how little his son and his son's friend's lives would be valued at if once they were found to be maintaining a slave camp.

Felton Tanner took a small pistol from the closet. It was a little twenty-two calibre muff pistol, modelled on a derringer. He had bought it for his wife years ago, but she had refused to carry it. 'No point in splashing his brains all round the room,' he remarked pragmatically, ''specially where Isaacs might be sniffing round tomorrow.' He slipped the gun into his jacket pocket and left the room. A moment later, Dave Tanner and Jack Lawrence heard his footsteps on the stairs as he headed up to the guestroom.

'Not worry the old folks about things!' said Jack Lawrence bitterly. 'Shows how much we know.'

'Hey, after all that, we forgot to tell my pa that Zeke Cartwright was in this very room,' Dave Tanner said. 'Maybe I ought to go up and tell him now?'

From overhead, there came the muffled crack of a small calibre weapon; the sort of sound which might be produced if a muff pistol were to be fired through a cushion or pillow.'

'I'm not sure he'd care all that much,' said Jack Lawrence.'

As they rode back towards Fort Crane, Ezekiel Cartwright came to a decision which he had been mulling over in his mind since leaving the kitchen at the Tanners' house. He said to the others, 'Rein in a moment.' When they had done so, he continued, 'Time's come for us all to part, I reckon.'

'Don't be crazy, man,' said Blake, 'you haven't yet had a chance to speak your piece to that old fellow. I thought that was the whole object of the exercise.'

Cartwright didn't feel called upon to explain himself and merely shrugged. He said, 'I'm a free man and I don't aim for to carry on to town.'

Sheriff Isaacs looked at him with irritation. 'You're

going to queer things for me, ain't that the case? Shee, just when things are starting to move.'

'I won't be made any man's cat's paw,' said Cartwright. 'You're using us for your own ends. I'll do what I will and I defy any man to stop me.'

It was a tricky situation for Albert Isaacs. What this awkward cuss said was quite true; there was no reason at all why he shouldn't go off on his own. Yet Isaacs knew in his water that this could wreck his own plans. He said, 'I'm more'n half minded to run you in on some other matter.'

'You can't do that,' said Enoch Blake, at once. 'It wouldn't be right and you know it.' Turning to Cartwright, he said, 'I'd hoped that we could ride this trail together.'

Cartwright shrugged. 'That's how it goes,' he said, 'but I'm obliged to you for your help, all the same.'

'What about that horse I fixed up for you?' asked Sheriff Isaacs.

'I'll bring it back when I'm done. I ain't going to rob you, nor commit no murder, neither. You both know that to be true.'

And so the sheriff and former sheriff made off towards Fort Crane, leaving Ezekiel Cartwright sitting on the horse that he had been loaned, watching them as they left.

'You reckon he'll return that horse?' asked Isaacs.

'Either that or die in the attempt,' replied his friend. 'I never met a straighter man in all my born days.'

*

As Jack Lawrence had guessed, when he was told that Cartwright had come to the house in company with the sheriff, Felton Tanner was not in the least degree alarmed. 'So what?' he asked contemptuously, 'You think I care about that damned cissie? He was weak then and I doubt a spell in gaol has altered him any. Never mind about him; what you boys after doing about the set-up out at the bluff?'

'We ain't given it a whole lot of thought,' said his son. 'This all only blew up today.'

The old man was rejoicing in the chance to take back a little of the power which he had felt ebbing away from him over the past year or two. He had no intention of being sidestepped this time. 'You never hear about striking while the iron's hot?' he asked. 'What say we ride out to the bluff this very minute and put the fear of God into those greasers once for all? You know as well as I do that just two men up there won't serve, not more than for a day or two, leastways. I reckon one of us'll have to stay there for a spell.'

The dismayed look on the faces of the other two as he suggested this was a pure delight to Felton Tanner. He had long ago sensed that neither of them cared over much to be spending too long up at the camp. They were too dainty by half; wanted the profits, but didn't like to get their hands dirty making the money. Well, he'd show 'em how it was done!

'Well, what say?' asked Felton Tanner. 'Cat got your tongues?'

Both of the younger men stood staring at this man in his eighties, who suddenly appeared to them to have more vim in him than the two of them together. Dave Tanner looked uncertainly to Jack Lawrence and said to his friend, 'What d'you think?'

'Never mind what he thinks,' said his father, 'you'd do better to mind what I think.'

On a hill overlooking the Tanners' house, Ezekiel Cartwright sat patiently, watching and waiting to see what might develop. His horse was tethered on the other side of the hill out of sight and he himself sat as still as a rock. He had been sitting there for upwards of an hour, when three men emerged from the house, took some tack from the barn and saddled up three horses which were grazing in a nearby field. Then they set off together in the general direction of a towering, rocky monolith which dominated the landscape. When he was sure that they were far enough advanced on their journey that none of them were about to turn back for something he might have forgotten, Cartwright mounted his own horse and proceeded at a leisurely pace down the hill, until he was by the house.

His calls for attention remaining unanswered, Cartwright dismounted and put his horse in the field. Then he went over to the door from which he had seen the men come and tried the handle. It opened at once and he went into the house to have a look around.

Nothing about any of these actions troubled Cartwright's conscience. He wasn't aiming to steal from the house and while he was invading their privacy, the greater good which might be achieved by Felton Tanner's repentance made that a matter of small moment. Cartwright knew that he would not be able to die easy if he hadn't at least given the man who had wronged him the opportunity to make some amends. At the very least, he would himself have to forgive the fellow face to face.

It had not been possible to see clearly the faces of those who had left the house and so there was a chance that Felton Tanner was still here; sleeping or resting, perhaps. Having checked the downstairs rooms, Cartwright went upstairs and in the first room, found the bloody corpse of a man who had been cruelly mutilated. Some of the blood was dried, but a fresh trickle ran from one of his ears. Whoever he was, he had been in a pitiful state before receiving the wound from which he had died.

CHAPTER 10

There was nothing to be done for the dead man and a quick look around the rest of the house soon showed that there was nobody else in the place. Ezekiel Cartwright stood and looked out a window on the top storey of the house, temporarily baffled. It was then that he saw three tiny, dark dots moving slowly along the side of the rocky bluff. It was too far to see any detail, but he was suddenly certain that those dots represented the three men who had left the house and ridden off in the direction of the huge pillar which jutted from the surrounding plain. For some reason, Cartwright had a premonition of evil and he shivered, as though somebody had walked across his grave. Then he muttered to himself, 'You fellows are up to no good and I'd take oath upon it.' He went downstairs and then left the house. Once outside, he mounted the horse which the sheriff had lent him and set out towards the bluff.

*

Sheriff Isaacs kept glancing back and when he was sure that Cartwright had moved on, said to his old friend, 'Just hold up now, Blake. Let's see where we are.'

Both men halted and Blake said, 'What have you in mind? I won't be party to anything against Cartwright, I tell you that straight.'

'Cartwright? I don't care a tinker's cuss about him. It's those Tanners I have in my sights. Something's happened there on their land and it might give me the leverage to crack open whatever game they're playing.'

'They looked spooked, I'll grant you that.'

'Listen, Cartwright said he was a free man and I'll allow as that's the truth. But that don't limit my actions in any wise whatever. He's going back to the Tanners' place, for a bet. No reason why we shouldn't head back there too.'

Enoch Blake thought over this idea and said at length, 'You're in the right. No reason at all. I've a notion that everything's reaching a point here. Maybe it'll work out for the best for Cartwright.'

'Cartwright! What is it with you and that fellow? Why does he matter so to you?'

'Because he's a good man and he's been cruelly wronged.'

Hearing such a blunt statement made Isaacs feel a little uncomfortable and he said, 'Yeah, yeah. There's a heap o' good men been wronged. That's the way of the world. You coming back with me?'

'I reckon.'

In the event, the two of them didn't reach the Tanners' house, for as they rode in that direction and crested the ridge of land which led down to the Tanners' and Lawrences' spread, Sheriff Isaacs exclaimed, 'Hallo, what's to do there?'

'What?'

'Over yonder. If that ain't the piebald I loaned that so-called friend of yours, then I'm a Dutchman. He's galloping hell for leather off towards the bluff.'

'Like we agreed, he's a free agent. It's nothing to us where he wants to ride.'

'True enough,' said Isaacs, 'but mark what I say, he's on the scent of something. He surely ain't riding that fast for the fun of it. Has he any other motive for what he's about? Other than confronting old man Tanner, that is?'

'No, that's all he cares about, from all that I'm able to collect.'

'Well then, he's got a lead on the man. I reckon we'll just tag along now.'

So it was that Dave Tanner and his father, accompanied by Jack Lawrence, were all three of them pursued by Ezekiel Cartwright; who was in turn being tracked by Sheriff Isaacs and his friend Enoch Blake. Had the circumstances been less deadly serious, then there might have been something irresistibly comic about the sight of those six men, all chasing one another up a little mountain. As it was, they none of them, for various reasons, felt in the slightest way inclined towards seeing the ridiculous aspect of the situation.

Dave Tanner was feeling ticked off at the way that his father had somehow managed, once more, to assume control of things that day. It was always the way. Whenever he had persuaded himself that his pa was utterly spent and no longer a force to be reckoned with, something of this sort happened and the old man took over once again.

When they were at the gate to the camp, Felton Tanner dismounted with an agility that belied his age and then snapped his fingers imperiously, saying, 'Key!' With an ill grace, his son handed down the key to the gate, which the old man then proceeded to unlock. The two overseers came rushing over to see what was to do. The old man growled testily, 'Mind what you're about with those rifles! I don't feel like getting shot today.'

When all three of them were safely in the mining camp, Felton Tanner marched across to the overseers and began to deal with them directly. His father, thought Tanner, really was determined to show who was in charge here today.

The two overseers looked on, a little awestruck to see the famous Felton Tanner in the flesh. Of late, the old man wasn't seen out and about much and this was the first time that they had actually met him. There was little time to gawp, though, because Felton Tanner demanded the rifle of one of the men. Once he had it in his hands, he checked it over carefully, before asking,

'Where's all these damned boys who've been causing so much to do?'

'They're in the tents, sir,' said one of the men obsequiously. 'You want I should show you the way?'

'I got eyes in my head, ain't I?'

It was no great study for Cartwright to discover the path which spiralled up around the side of the bluff. He thought it wise to dismount and make his way up on foot, figuring that he could approach more quietly that way. Not that he felt any need to tiptoe about, but one man had already been killed just lately and there was no percentage in barging in and inviting somebody to shoot him.

He was in good condition, but even so felt a mite breathless by the time he reached the barbed wire fence with an open gate. Three horses stood near this gate and a little way across an open area, Cartwright could see a row of army tents. There was something sinister about the place, although he couldn't precisely say what. As he stood there, he heard voices coming from the tents and then a cry of pain. There was dirty business being undertaken here; of that he had no doubt at all. One of the horses pawing the ground a few feet away had a scabbard hanging alongside the saddle, with the stock of a weapon protruding from it. When Cartwright reached it out, he found that it was a scattergun with the barrel shortened to a foot or so. It was an old percussion lock weapon, but there were caps under the nipples and it was evidently charged. Such a gun would do well enough for close-up work and he would just have to hope that nobody was going to lay an ambush for him from more than twenty-five yards or so. A weapon like that, with a shortened barrel, lost its force dramatically after a few yards. From the tents came another scream of pain. It sounded like a child's cry.

There were seven youths in one of the tents and another six in the next. Altogether, there were enough tents and bunks for thirty workers, but the camp had never yet worked at such a capacity. Felton Tanner had a basic knowledge of Spanish, picked up from the times in his youth when he rode with comancheros and also lived for a spell in Mexico. He had announced as soon as he entered the tent that he was going to kill one of the boys there, but that he hadn't yet decided which one. The youngsters were secured to their bunks by a stout chain which ran through the shackles on their ankles and was threaded through the wood of the bunks themselves. They would have needed to dismantle every bunk before it was possible to leave the tent.

After making his announcement, the old man walked along the line of bunks and, giving no warning of his intention, had swung the rifle hard against the shins of one boy, who gave a sharp cry of pain. Then Tanner continued strolling along the bunks, relishing the terror that he was creating. He hadn't yet decided if he really was going to kill anybody or not. After the four deaths among the workers that day, it would of course be a matter of some urgency to recruit new men and rush them here from New Orleans. That being so, it seemed to Felton Tanner that it might be a salutary lesson to these scum to see how cheap their lives were valued by killing one or two in front of the others. After all, a crew of eleven was not that much different from a crew of thirteen.

The fact of the matter was that the old man was having a whale of a time, making these young men afraid of him. He had always enjoyed seeing fear in the faces of those he was robbing or attacking, but as he grew older there had been fewer and fewer opportunities to indulge this vice. Felton Tanner meant to make the most of his fun that day. He was so engrossed in the overwhelmingly pleasurable occupation of frightening a bunch of young men who were little more than boys, that he quite failed to notice that another person had entered the tent and was now standing behind the four men who were watching him with appalled fascination.

Dave Tanner had known from a child that his father enjoyed tormenting those weaker and more vulnerable than himself. He had had ample proof of this tendency as he grew up. Similarly, Jack Lawrence knew what the old man could be like when given his head. The other two, though, knew nothing of all this and although tough and unpleasant enough characters in their own right, thought that there was something unsavoury and unappetizing about the spectacle of somebody of that age terrorizing a bunch of boys. They were neither of them minded to interfere, though, as they knew what side their bread was buttered on. If their two bosses were content to allow this old fellow to carry on so, then who were they to object?

Because the men standing just inside the tent, watching the old man's antics, were so bound up in the sight, they didn't even hear Zeke Cartwright, not until he said quietly, 'You men best not move a muscle now. I got a scattergun aiming right at you and at this range, I couldn't hardly miss.'

None of the four men felt inclined to put the matter to the test as they turned slowly round to see who was speaking. Felton Tanner was too busy aiming the rifle at some boy's face and pretending that he was going to pull the trigger, to see what was happening behind him.

'I already taken first pull,' Cartwright informed them in a conversational tone, 'and if I so much as tense up, then I reckon we'll all be sorry.'

Dave Tanner said, 'What d'you want, Cartwright?'

'What I want is a few words with your pa. But first I want to know what wickedness is going on here. All of you just drop your weapons on the ground. I can tell you, at this range, I let fly with both barrels and at least two of you'll be tore in half. The others'll take longer to die, but I reckon I'd account for every one of you.'

The thing that all of them marked was that there was not only a complete absence of bravado about the man, but he was also utterly lacking in any fear. This is an alarming circumstance when a man's drawing down on you with a shotgun, because it means whatever you do, it probably won't be enough to stop him firing. They all of them had had enough experience of such matters to realize that the only sensible dodge right now was to do just as they were bid and to let fall their guns. When one of the overseers had cast down his rifle and the others had drawn their pistols and dropped them in the dirt, Cartwright called over to Felton Tanner, saying, 'It's been nigh on forty years, Tanner. I got words to bandy with you.'

Tanner looked round in surprise, taking in the situation at a glance. He saw that his son and the others were covered by an old man holding a scattergun on them. 'Why, you soft fool,' he cried, 'what makes you to come up here?' He was not so injudicious as to point the rifle at Cartwright, but neither did he relinquish hold of it; just kept it loosely in his hands so that he could bring it up to aim if the chance should present itself. He knew that he could do nothing at present without casting the life of his own son into hazard.

'What's to do, Cartwright?' asked Felton Tanner. 'I saw where you were only lately let out. Why've you come haring up here?'

'Tell you the truth, I don't think I need have bothered,' said Cartwright sadly. 'I was hoping you might have repented of setting me up to hang. From what I seen this day, I'd guess that's by way of being what they term a forlorn hope.'

'You got that right. You'd have better stayed in Milledgeville, you fool.'

'Well then, just stop troubling those boys and put down your rifle. I got something to say to you, all the same.'

Felton Tanner thought about this for a moment and then said, 'You let those others go first. They have no part in this.'

The truth was that Ezekiel Cartwright had not the least intention of shooting the men he was currently holding at gunpoint. His only wish was to make his peace with the man who had stolen so many years of his life. With eternity before him, Cartwright didn't aim to enter into the presence of the Lord with any grudges or ill feelings from the world still tainting him. If only people weren't so suspicious, he could have dealt with this in a matter of seconds, just explained to Tanner that he freely forgave him and hoped that the man would in time feel some remorse, for the sake of his own soul. Since passing through that barbed wire fence, though, Cartwright had realized that something filthy was going on and that these poor young devils were in need of rescuing. He could see that they were bound with chains and even without knowing the full details, he was aware that it was his duty to set them all free. It was a blessed nuisance, because he had wished to spend the last weeks of his life at rest after speaking to Tanner. He said out loud, 'Listen, you four, I got no interest in any of you. I've a suspicion that you're all up to your elbows in something dirty here, but we'll think on that later. For now, I want to speak to that old man.'

Dave Tanner and Jack Lawrence exchanged looks that indicated that they were minded to jump him and so Cartwright said, 'Don't do it, fellows. Any mistake with this here gun ain't likely to be put right in this world, you hear what I'm saying? I don't aim to harm that Felton Tanner. Just want to say something to him in private.'

'Do as he says,' said the old man, 'he's a pussy cat. He ain't got it in him to hurt a fly. Go on, now. I can handle this.'

With some reluctance, Dave Tanner did as his father instructed him, favouring Cartwright with a hard stare as he went. The two overseers had not the faintest idea what was going on, but decided that they had best simply do as they had been told.

After Cartwright and Tanner were left in the tent with the Mexican boys, there was silence for a short time, before the older of the two men said harshly, 'Well, let's hear it. You waited forty years to say it, so let it out. Or maybe you really aim to kill me all along. Let's have it, then.'

Keeping the scattergun vaguely turned in the other man's direction, although more pointed upwards than anything, Ezekiel Cartwright shook his head and said wonderingly, 'I had time enough to think about what you did to me. Since I been saved by the blood of Jesus,

I been praying that you're not as bad as I once thought. Making excuses for you in my mind, you know. Now I see you, what you're up to here and all, I see I was wrong. You're a worse man than I ever dreamed.'

'That it?' asked Felton Tanner, his voice contemptuous. 'All you could come up with in those years in gaol? Like I always said, you were gullible and soft. Deserved to be took advantage of.'

Cartwright looked at Felton Tanner with an infinite expression upon his face. 'You poor devil,' he said pityingly, 'I came all this way just to let you know that I forgive you for what you done. No more than that. And I do, what's more. For all that I suffered, I reckon I got the best of the deal. Leastways, my soul's my own and I hope to die easy. Lord knows what a weight of sin you'll take with you when you breathe your last. But I do forgive you. I wanted you to know.'

'You got aught else to say?'

'Now you happened to mention it, there's one more thing. Now that I am here.'

'What's that?'

'You can just turn these boys loose of their bonds. I don't know what's going on here, but I tell you now, I don't like the look of it.'

Felton Tanner gave no reply to this peremptory request, but simply stood staring back at Cartwright.

Sheriff Isaacs and Enoch Blake found the horse that Zeke Cartwright had been loaned standing at the foot of the path leading up the bluff. There was no sign of

Cartwright, though. 'I'd say at a guess,' opined Isaacs, 'that we'll find that Cartwright up there, closeted with the Tanners and maybe Jack Lawrence. What the devil's going on?'

'We've heard no shooting,' said Blake, 'so whatever it is, they've not yet fallen out over it.'

'Even so, I reckon we should get up there and see what's what.'

Like Cartwright, Isaacs and Blake left their horses at the foot of the path and set off on foot, in order to alert nobody of their imminent arrival. For the sheriff, this was a chance to solve a little mystery which had been nagging away at him for quite some time. Blake's only motive was to lend a hand, if he could, to Ezekiel Cartwright; a man he had come to consider as something very rare and special. It wasn't every day that one met a true Christian and Blake was not about to let any harm befall such a person if he could help it. The two of them were halfway up the path, plodding along patiently and silently, when they heard the crack of a rifle shot. This ominous sound was followed almost immediately by the dull boom of a scattergun. They abandoned the attempt to creep up quietly; drawing their pistols and breaking into a sprint.

Felton Tanner had not the least idea of releasing the slaves, but did not think it wise to declare this openly while facing down a man with a sawn-off shotgun in his hands; no matter how much he thought that the fellow wouldn't shoot. Instead, he temporized, saying,

'I ain't got the key to this chain. You'd have to ask my son.'

'And turn my back on you? Don't think it for a second.'

Most people in such a tense and dangerous position would be scared out of their wits, but for old Felton Tanner, the whole thing was an invigorating break from the dull routine of his recent existence. Truth to tell, he was having the time of his life. It was many years since he had been mixed up in any such lively action. So intoxicating was this sudden outburst of violence that the old man took it into his head to take decisive, if risky, measures to end the confrontation between him and the man he had condemned to four decades of a living hell. Being pretty sure that Cartwright was too soft to be a real menace, Tanner brought the rifle that he was holding up to his shoulder with the intention of putting a bullet through this troublesome intruder's heart. He might have succeeded, for he was still a deadly shot, except that one of the Mexicans saw what he was about and lashed out with his foot as the rifle went up, spoiling Felton Tanner's aim.

Instead of ploughing its way through Cartwright's chest, the ball instead grazed his upper right arm; he felt as though a red hot poker had been pressed against his flesh. His hand twitched convulsively, causing him to loose off one of the barrels of the scattergun, filling the tent with a deafening roar. Cartwright hadn't been aiming the piece anywhere in particular, having been in the habit when he was a youth of keeping any weapon that he was holding pointing up at the sky until he was ready to use it. It was the kind of elementary precaution which prevented accidental injuries and death. The only effect of the shot was accordingly to rip a wide hole in the canvas above his head.

Cartwright's reactions were as sharp as those of a man half his age. As soon as the exchange of fire had taken place, he dropped instantly to the ground, rolling under one of the bunks for cover. The Mexican boys, perhaps hoping to spook Felton Tanner, to whom they had taken a great dislike, began shouting and rattling their chains. This created a chaotic atmosphere which was not conducive to calm and reasoned thought. One thing Ezekiel Cartwright knew was that his first duty was to help those poor, starved youngsters. He surely did not wish to harm anybody, but that might be the lesser of two evils. It was possible that he would have to shoot those who were running this dreadful place in order to free these captives. So be it.

CHAPTER 11

As Sheriff Isaacs and Enoch Blake reached the narrow cleft, which was blocked by a barbed wire fence, they heard more shooting. Two men were standing near the fence with their backs to them as they passed through the open gate. Isaacs said loudly, 'You men, what's going on here?'

'Lordy, Sheriff,' said one of them, a fellow Isaacs recognized from having seen around time sometimes, 'this ain't nothin' to do with us.' Both he and his friend looked as though they had been caught unawares and were terrified out of their wits, which was indeed the case.

Isaacs said, 'You boys stand right there and don't even think of moving. I know the both of you.'

There came the sound of pistol fire from a row of tents twenty yards or so from them and Isaacs and Blake ran to see what was happening.

From his vantage point on the ground, Cartwright saw that he was close to the guns that the other men had discarded at his orders. He reached out and took up a forty-five pistol. Old Felton Tanner was calling out, taunting him. He said, 'That all you can do after those years in the pen? Forgive me? Are you a man or what?'

There was the crack of another rifle shot and Cartwright worried that if he didn't put the old sinner out of action soon, one of the chained up boys was apt to stop a ball. He raised his hand above the bunk and fired over Tanner's head, shouting after he had done so, 'Give up those men, Tanner. I give you my oath, I ain't after pursuing you. You can go to the devil for all I care. Just let those boys loose.'

'All right,' shouted back Felton Tanner, 'you stand up and show yourself. Let's parlay.'

Before he was able to think of an appropriate answer to this suggestion, there came the sound of a shot behind him and Cartwright felt a dull blow to his back. He knew at once that he'd been hit. Instinct took over, causing him to forget all his religious beliefs and he whirled round and snapped off a couple of shots at the man who had crept into the tent behind him. Dave Tanner leapt to his feet with a look of the most profound surprise on his face at being shot. Then he glanced down at the two neat little holes in the front of his chest, moved his lips as though he was about to say something and then dropped dead, not fifteen feet from Cartwright.

Felton Tanner might have been a dyed-in-the-wool

villain, but at least he had the saving grace of being inordinately fond of his own flesh and blood. On seeing his beloved only son fall dead, the old man gave a howl of rage and grief and began running down the space between the bunks towards his son. Three things then happened, so quickly, that afterwards the Mexicans, who had been witnesses to the whole scene, were unable to agree with each other on the definite order of events.

When the sound of shooting came from the tent, Dave Tanner had been fearful for his father's safety and had rushed forward without more ado. Jack Lawrence had hung back for a second, not being so fond of old Mr Tanner that he was prepared to lay down his life for him. So it was that Dave Tanner entered the tent just after Zeke Cartwright had fired a wild shot in the general direction of his father. He couldn't be expected to know that the last thing that Cartwright had on his mind was murder and scarcely listened to the shouted exchange between Cartwright and his pa. He saw that the gun he had earlier abandoned still lay where he had dropped it and it was the work of a moment to snatch it up and shoot Cartwright in the back.

Jack Lawrence had decided that he should after all support his oldest friend and so moved forward and ducked under the flap of the tent, but just as he did so, his arm was gripped from behind and the cold muzzle of a pistol was pressed to his neck. He heard the voice of the sheriff of Fort Crane say softly, 'Don't you move a muscle, friend, or you're as good as dead.' He froze, having no reason to doubt that Albert Isaacs meant just exactly what he said.

While Isaacs held one man at gunpoint, Enoch Blake pressed into the tent, anxious to find the man who he had promised himself to take care of. He was just in time to see a crazy-looking old man running towards him with a rifle in his hand, screaming that he would kill him. This at least was the construction that Blake put upon the old man's threat, although he later worked out that the words had actually been directed at Ezekiel Cartwright. It was a split-second decision and Blake chose to take the fellow's words at face value and so he shot Felton Tanner in the belly, causing him to tumble forward and then fall flat on his face, losing his hold on the rifle as he did so. Blake stepped forward at once and kicked the rifle out of the fallen man's reach.

There didn't seem to be anybody else aiming to kill him and there was no more shooting. Blake looked round the tent and shivered involuntarily at the sight of the youngsters chained to the bunks. He knew at once that something evil had been going on, although he couldn't yet work out what. While casting his eyes around, he saw Cartwright, sitting on the ground and slumped against one of the bunks. The man's face was pale and he appeared to be breathing with some difficulty. His arm was dripping with blood. Squatting down in front of the wounded man, Blake said, 'Hey. How's it going?'

'Depends what you mean. I'm bound for glory, I reckon.'

'Don't say so,' said Blake, stricken with a feeling of grief, for all that he had only known this remarkable man for a few days. He said, 'Let me have a look now. You hit anywhere other than that arm?'

'Don't trouble yourself, Blake. I took a ball in my back. I'm not long for this world, I'm thankful to say.'

'Don't talk if it tires you.'

From near at hand, came a querulous and angry voice. It was Felton Tanner saying, 'You bastard. You shot me. Straight through my belly. It's like to be mortal, you son of a bitch.'

Blake said quietly to Ezekiel Cartwright, 'Just a moment. I've something to attend to.' He stood up and walked over to where Tanner lay in a growing pool of blood. Looking down at the old man, Blake said, 'You done killed my friend.'

'What, that Cartwright? He didn't have no friends. Spent the last forty years locked up.'

''Cause o' you.'

'So what? What's it matter to you? Get me to a doctor.'

From his vantage point, Enoch Blake could see what the old man could not, that the speed at which the pool of blood was spreading meant that the wounded man would bleed to death in another few minutes. He said, 'Sure I'll get you to a doctor. But only if you tell me the truth about Cartwright. You set him up, ain't that right?'

'Yes, yes. It was long ago. I'm sorry, all right? Just get me to a doctor. Hurry, man!'

'You hear that, Isaacs?' called Blake over his shoulder.

'I heard,' said the sheriff, 'happen you were right about that fellow all along.'

Blake left Felton Tanner complaining with decreasing vigour as the blood drained from his body and went back to see how Cartwright was. He knelt down by the injured man and said gently, 'How you feeling now?'

Cartwright managed a wry smile and replied, 'I won't be sorry to be out of this. I'm going home.'

It was hardly a time for polite fictions and so Blake didn't trouble to try and disabuse the man of the idea that he was dying. Instead he said, 'Is there aught I can do for you?'

'One thing you could do.'

'Name it.'

'For most of my life folk've looked at me like I'm something lower than a cockroach. I'd sure like to think that after I go, the truth about me comes out. That I had no part in that filthy crime all them years ago.'

'You got it. Anything else?'

'No. Thanks for your help. I reckon I'll sleep now.' Having said which, Ezekiel Cartwright closed his eyes and his breathing grew slower and deeper, as though he was in truth simply drifting off to sleep. Blake watched for a time and then stood up and went to see how Felton

Tanner was doing, because the old man's complaints and cursing had grown fainter and stopped. The explanation was simple; the man had died of massive loss of blood.

Sheriff Isaacs was standing with his prisoner, the man Blake understood to be a Mr Lawrence. He went up to the two of them and said to Jack Lawrence, 'What is this place? Don't bother lying, it won't serve.'

'Gold mine,' replied Lawrence shortly.

'These men'd be the miners, I'm guessing?'

Jack Lawrence shrugged, he was clearly coming to terms with the fact that he would most likely be standing trial for various capital crimes before too long. There was a mulish obstinacy about the fellow's face, which led Blake to suspect that the man had hopes of buying his way out of this trouble, either by paying for some slick lawyer or by straightforward bribery of jurors or some such trick.

Blake bent down to check on Cartwright and found that he had stopped breathing. At least his sufferings were at an end and he had gone to his Lord. He stood up and said to the sheriff, 'You want I try and cut a deal with those other two?'

Because he'd worked with Albert Isaacs on one or two previous cases in the past, Blake didn't need to spell out just precisely what he meant. Isaacs nodded and Enoch Blake left the tent to speak to the two men who were standing just exactly where they had been left. Although his natural impulse was to knock them down or even shoot them for their part in what he was beginning to suppose to be a dreadful crime, Blake forced a cheerful smile on his face and said simply, 'Either of you fellows happen to have keys to those chains?' Both men fell over themselves in their haste to comply with this request. When he had the key, Blake turned as though to leave. Then he swung back suddenly and asked, 'Which of you men will turn state's evidence?'

There was a pause and then one of the men said eagerly, 'I'll do it! I'll tell you all you want.'

'So will I,' said the other of the men, 'I'll cooperate.'

'That's right good to hear,' said Blake sardonically. 'I'll tell the sheriff that you both are keen to help him.'

As he made his way back to Isaacs, Enoch Blake didn't trouble to tell the men that he had no official standing whatever and that Sheriff Isaacs could quite legally ignore any offer that Blake had made. With luck, Isaacs would get a deal of information from those two men, while they were under the impression that they had been granted some sort of immunity from prosecution. He'd leave Isaacs to handle those details.

Sheriff Isaacs said, 'Any luck?'

'Oh, yes. You want I should free these poor devils?'

'Go right ahead. They're all material witnesses, so we'll need to get them somewhere to stay.' His face brightened and he said, 'Say, the Tanner place'll be empty! Maybe they could stay there.'

After the young men had been freed from the

bunks, they stood up and came over to where Ezekiel Cartwright was still sitting against one of the bunks. Having seen how Felton Tanner had behaved towards them, and realizing that Cartwright was opposed in some way to him, they looked down at him with respect. One or two crossed themselves and murmured prayers for the repose of the man who they supposed had been instrumental in rescuing them.

Jack Lawrence had decided that his best policy lay in keeping his moth altogether shut, what they called 'reserving his defence'. Blake hoped fervently that it would do the man no good. He said to the sheriff, 'I'll willingly lend a hand straightening matters out here for a day or two. I'd be greatly obliged, though, if you could see your way to leaving my name out your report. Don't want to be coming back and forth to appear in court and suchlike. I'd say you got enough evidence without that.'

'Yeah, I reckon I can do that. Let's get this place cleared up now.'

'One more thing. You heard what that old bastard said before he died. You'll use official channels to help clear Cartwright's name?'

'Can't see as it matters after all this time. Still, if it matters all that much to you, then I'll lend a hand, sure.'

Together, the two men, ably assisted by the former overseers, labouring under the delusion that they were not going to be arrested and charged with slaving and complicity in murder, helped the Mexicans to understand that they were free and were about to be taken somewhere safe. Then the whole party set off on foot along the path down the bluff, some of the boys leading the horses.

When they reached the bottom, they paused for a moment and Blake said to the sheriff, 'It ain't every day you meet a really good man.'

'Which may be true,' replied Isaacs, 'but we still got to get this mess sorted out.'

Together, the sheriff and former sheriff began shepherding their charges along the track, in the direction of what had once been the Tanners' house.

Enoch Blake thought that it would have been a scurvy trick to play on Sheriff Isaacs, simply to fetch up in his town, set off a powder keg and then go scuttling off back home again. After all, the violent events that day would never have taken place had he not brought Ezekiel Cartwright to Fort Crane. The consequence was that he offered to stay on in town for a few days, until matters were well in hand. 'I reckon that's the right thing,' Isaacs responded. 'Mind, you done me a favour, really. I been watching those rascals for a time, without once guessing what they were about. But I'd appreciate your help and I'm thankful for it.'

It took the Mexican boys some time to realize that they truly had been liberated. When they finally understood that they were going to be staying in the Tanners' well-appointed house, their amazement was pleasant to behold. Jack Lawrence watched sourly as the crowd of ragged and ill-kempt greasers swarmed into his old friend's childhood home, but he said nothing.

As the cavalcade consisting of Sheriff Isaacs, Blake, Jack Lawrence and the two overseers entered town, there were raised eyebrows and considerable interest in the sight. Having settled the Mexicans into the Tanners' house and made it clear that they were safe and would be looked after, Sheriff Isaacs thought it prudent to tie the hands of his three prisoners, lashing their wrists together in front of them so they could still ride. He didn't want to lose any of them. Seeing Lawrence and two men, who were familiar in town, being held prisoner a man called from the boardwalk, 'What's to do, Sheriff?'

'Never you mind,' replied Isaacs repressively. 'Official business is all.'

When they got to the sheriff's office, the two overseers cavilled a little at the idea of being locked in the cells, still under the delusion that they were going to walk away scot-free from the affair, but Enoch Blake reassured them, saying, 'You two make your statements to the sheriff this very day and I make no doubt we'll have it all cleared up in next to no time.' Had they been a little more astute, the men might have remarked that Sheriff Isaacs himself had said nothing about any deal; had in fact remained studiously aloof from any hand in the conversation. At a later date, this would enable him to swear on oath that he had offered none of his prisoners any inducement to give statements and that they had done so of their own free will. It was hardly his fault if somebody with no official standing at all had been promising them a lot of foolishness!

Before the sun set that day, the men who had actually been running the camp had provided enough evidence to put ropes around not only their own necks, but also that belonging to Jack Lawrence. Cheerfully, they signed their names to the statements, expecting to be promptly released on their own recognisance. The look of dismay on their faces when the sheriff proceeded to charge both them and Jack Lawrence with enslavement, complicity in murder and depriving various men of their civil rights was almost comical.

After a few days of riding to and fro to the Tanners' house, helping with the excavations up at the mining camp – which unearthed no fewer than fourteen bodies in shallow graves – and various other matters, Enoch Blake decided that he had repaid any debt he owed to the sheriff of Fort Crane. Before he saddled up and left the town, he said to his old friend, 'Touching upon that other matter, that of clearing Cartwright's name, you've not forgot that, I'm hopeful to think?'

'I'm sending a wire to the governor's office in the next few days.'

'Think that'll answer?'

'With my statement about hearing that old rogue's admission? Yeah, I'd say it's certain sure.'

So it proved, because two months after he returned

to his farm, Blake saw, on visiting Atlanta one day, that the newspapers there were full of two pieces of sensational news. The first was that slavery had returned to one corner of the south and that three men had been convicted of their parts in the crime, as well as a number of counts of murder. All were due to hang within the week. The second piece of news was of interest chiefly to older citizens of the town, who might recollect the great gold robbery of 1849, a crime which had been accompanied by a most atrocious series of murders. It appeared beyond doubt that the man gaoled for this terrible crime had been proved, beyond the shadow of a doubt, to be quite innocent and that the governor of Georgia had granted him a posthumous pardon.

When he got back from Atlanta, Blake showed his sister and daughter the newspaper, remarking that the man who had stayed at their home had now been fully exonerated. He also broached the more delicate topic of possibly leaving the farm. His little escapade in Fort Crane had given him more satisfaction than he had ever found in a year's tilling the soil. Old friends in Atlanta had urged him to sign up as a marshal, assuring him that the service was crying out for experienced men such as him.

He was gratified that both Izzie and Catherine were wholly in favour of moving to Atlanta and so that was all right as well. As he went to make the necessary preliminary preparations for leaving, Enoch Blake reflected that Cartwright's release had triggered many changes in the world and all of them good. It was, he felt, a fitting enough epitaph for a man who had suffered so many wrongs.